W9-BMU-033

# Caught

## ROBBIE MICHAELS

Harmony Ink

Published by
HARMONY INK PRESS

5032 Capital Circle SW, Suite 2, PMB# 279, Tallahassee, FL 32305-7886 USA
publisher@harmonyinkpress.com • http://harmonyinkpress.com

This is a work of fiction. Names, characters, places, and incidents either are the product of author imagination or are used fictitiously, and any resemblance to actual persons, living or dead, business establishments, events, or locales is entirely coincidental.

Caught
© 2014 Robbie Michaels.

Cover Art
© 2014 Bree Archer.
http://www.breearcher.com
Cover content is for illustrative purposes only and any person depicted on the cover is a model.

All rights reserved. This book is licensed to the original purchaser only. Duplication or distribution via any means is illegal and a violation of international copyright law, subject to criminal prosecution and upon conviction, fines, and/or imprisonment. Any eBook format cannot be legally loaned or given to others. No part of this book may be reproduced or transmitted in any form or by any means, electronic or mechanical, including photocopying, recording, or by any information storage and retrieval system, without the written permission of the Publisher, except where permitted by law. To request permission and all other inquiries, contact Harmony Ink Press, 5032 Capital Circle SW, Suite 2, PMB# 279, Tallahassee, FL 32305-7886, USA, or publisher@harmonyinkpress.com.

ISBN: 978-1-63216-594-7
Library Edition ISBN: 978-1-63216-595-4
Digital ISBN: 978-1-63216-596-1
Library of Congress Control Number: 2014948410
First Edition December 2014
Library Edition March 2015

Printed in the United States of America
∞
This paper meets the requirements of
ANSI/NISO Z39.48-1992 (Permanence of Paper).

# Chapter One
# Caught

WHEN MY dad unexpectedly barged into my bedroom that Friday night, he could not possibly have chosen a more inappropriate moment. What he walked in on was me and my best friend, Mark, going at it on top of my bed. One minute I was in heaven, lying on my back with Mark's sweet lips on mine, his tongue exploring my mouth and mine his, his hard dick poking me through his jeans, his hands on my head and in my hair. It was just the two of us, alone in the dark quiet of my bedroom, and life was good.

Then suddenly the world exploded, and I think my heart stopped beating for a minute from the shock. With no warning, my bedroom door swung open, my dad called my name, the overhead light was turned on, and Dad was looking at us. The bulb in that overhead light had to be a thousand-watt bulb, because it felt as if we were under an intense searchlight, something a ship at sea would use when looking for something. I couldn't remember it ever putting out so much light before. I was a prisoner in custody with the brightest of bright lights aimed my way so I had no hope of escape.

It was a toss-up as to who felt more surprised. Mark flew off first me and then the bed faster than seemed humanly possible. I heard him hit the wall. If the wall hadn't been there, I'm sure he would have kept going. But he did connect with it, so there he stood. My first reaction in the split second after it happened was to miss those sweet lips and the feel of his dick against me. My own erection was rivaling Mark's. I felt as if I could pound nails into a board with mine. But one look at my father's eyes, as wide open as I could recall ever seeing them, and I quickly lost my erection. I didn't check Mark, but I would have bet big money his was gone also.

I propped myself up on my elbows, quietly freaking out that we'd been caught. I really thought the world was ending. All my years of efforts to hide my sexuality were erased in an instant. Everything I'd tried to hide was no longer secret but now out there for the entire world to see. All the times Mark and I had held off doing or saying something for fear someone might see or hear us—all those times had been for nothing because it was all out there.

At least we were both dressed—mostly. I mean, we hadn't been that stupid to get all naked and rut around like a couple of animals. Sure, we'd wanted to—desperately wanted to—but all we'd been doing was kissing. We'd waited until a time when we thought we were in the house all by ourselves, a time when everyone was finally out somewhere. We'd closed the door to my bedroom, and we'd been quiet. What was the big deal? All right, I'll admit that my hands had found their way inside the back of Mark's jeans. Maybe I'd loosened his belt first so I could cup his gorgeous ass. But that was all.

My eyes darted around the room. It was my bedroom. I recognized everything in it. I'd seen it all, touched it all, and moved every single thing in it around at some point or another. It was my room, and it was as familiar to me as anything was. But it was also all different now. Nothing had been moved, but nothing was familiar any longer.

It felt like an eternity that we were frozen in place. I lay there, Mark stood there, and my dad stood there, all of us staring at one another but no one speaking. What was I supposed to say anyway? Coming out was off the table now, since my dad had figured out I was gay by the way Mark lay on top of me, kissing me like there was no tomorrow. Maybe there wasn't going to be a tomorrow.

I'm not sure why, but I had become surprisingly composed. I had absolutely zero reason to feel calm. I probably should still have been freaking as much as Mark, but for some inexplicable reason, all my panic had drained away. I just didn't seem to be panicked. Whatever the reason for my composure, for the moment I was able to focus on the situation somewhat logically.

My dad had a commanding presence. He was not a big guy. He only stood about five-five in height and was fairly trim, so he did not present an imposing figure. But a lot of energy, opinion, and ego were packed into that small frame. I'd always thought of him as something like a Great Dane or a Doberman in the body of a Chihuahua. If he'd ever heard me say something like that, he probably would have threatened to kick my ass, but that was just one of the many things about me that he didn't or shouldn't know. And unfortunately that list was one item shorter now.

I got my height from him. Or should I say, I got my lack of height from him. Usually a kid looks somewhat like one parent or another in some obvious way. But I was a blending of my parents. I got my height from my dad. I got my hair color from my mom. She's also the one who gave me my blue eyes. My trimness came from him, as did my nose, but my mom gave me my square jaw—my dad's was more the typical V-shaped jawline.

For someone who was usually loud and boisterous, that evening my dad looked—I don't know—blank, maybe? I couldn't figure out what was going to happen because I couldn't get a read on him. He just stood there and stared at us. Okay, so maybe it wasn't us. He stared at me. Me. I was the focus of his attention. He wasn't acting like himself in any way I'd ever seen.

I'd expected him to yell, rant, threaten, throw something, or punch something—probably me. Hell, I wished he'd done one of those things. Maybe not the punching part, but any of the rest. As I realized he wasn't going to scream and shout, I started to get scared. Mouthy Dad I could deal with—I'd dealt with him for seventeen-plus years. But Quiet Dad? No way. I didn't know him, and I didn't know what to expect from him.

I heard Mark panting like a trapped animal off to my right somewhere, but my entire focus was on my dad. Mark I could deal with in a minute, but my dad—this was bad. Without a word, Dad backed out of the room, and we heard his footsteps retreat back down the hall.

If he'd yelled at us I would have felt bad, but at least I would have known exactly what was on his mind. I knew he'd never be happy having a gay son. He'd never said that in so many words, but I knew him. He was a conservative man, financially and otherwise. He wouldn't approve. Hell, what father wanted a gay son? When asked what they wanted for their sons when they grew up, no fathers ever said, "I want my boy to be gay." It just didn't happen.

Mark hadn't moved. He still stood off to my right cowering against the wall, his eyes darting rapidly back and forth from the door to the window, seemingly analyzing which was the best way for him to make his escape. I felt bad for him. We'd talked about this night forever it seemed, and to have this happen just when we were getting started—well that just plain sucked. And Mark had been one damned fine kisser too. If his other sexual skills were anything like his kissing, then the sex we might have shared would have been smoking hot.

With Dad out of the room, it was time to focus on Mark. I swung my legs over the side of the bed and took a couple of steps toward him. He looked totally panicked. He looked like one of those deer caught crossing the wrong road at the wrong time on the wrong night. The look in his eyes was like that deer's, sort of "Oh shit!" The only difference was that the car hadn't hit him but had stopped and then backed up.

Close to him but not touching, I asked, "Are you okay?"

"What?" he demanded quietly. "What the fuck do you think? No! I'm not okay!" He closed his eyes and shook his head vigorously and just said, "This is bad. Oh, this is so bad." He kept repeating those words for a minute, all the while shaking his head. His beautiful skin had lost all its color. He looked pale and shaky. Crap. This wasn't just bad for my life; it could also be bad for Mark and his life.

Since Mark and I had been friends for years, my dad knew him and his parents. So I guessed I shouldn't have been surprised when Mark asked suddenly, "He's gonna tell my folks, isn't he?" He looked panicked and sounded almost breathless.

"Mark, dude, take a breath. We don't know anything. I don't know what he's thinking. Maybe he won't have a problem with this. Besides, if he does, his problem is gonna be with me."

"But my folks know your folks. They talk. They're gonna talk about this. You know they will. Crap. Crap. Crap. Why did this have to happen? Why did I come over here tonight? Fuck. I should have just gone home. Then you wouldn't have been kissing me, and he wouldn't have walked in on us."

It took me a couple of seconds of thinking about that statement to get really pissed. Sure, I wasn't happy about how this had fallen out, but Mark's phrasing put the whole fault—if there was any—on me. "Um, excuse me, but don't you mean that *we* were kissing? As I remember it, you were lying *on top* of me."

Mark suddenly reached up and shoved me away from him—hard. I hadn't been prepared for that move, so I tumbled backward. Fortunately I didn't hit anything as I went down, but I fell to the floor, yelling out in surprise as I went.

Mark, for his part, seemed oblivious. "I've got to get out of here," he yelled to the room overall.

"Mark! Baby. Chill," I told him as I jumped back to my feet. For the moment I was going to forget the fact that he'd just shoved me away. I didn't like it, but he had a temporary pass. I placed myself between him and the door and tried to get him to stop so we could talk this out and decide how to handle the situation, but I never even got to start.

"Don't touch me!" Mark yelled. So much for our whispered conversation. "I've got to get out of here," he repeated.

My anger was growing as he started for the door. I was half tempted to let him go as he was, but I couldn't do that. "Um, don't you want to zip up, buckle your belt, and put your shoes back on?" Rather than take my advice genially, Mark instead sneered at me, but at least he did what I recommended. He didn't look at all happy as he grabbed his shoes and shoved his feet into them without sitting down like he would normally do. Why was he so pissed at me? It wasn't his dad who had walked in on us in his bedroom. No, it was my dad in my bedroom. If anyone should be freaking out, it should be me. I didn't get why his response was so out of proportion to the moment.

"Where'd your dad go?" he demanded.

"How the hell should I know?" I asked him. "I haven't been anywhere you haven't."

And he shoved me again, snarling at me, "Don't say that."

"What?" I half begged, half demanded. What the fuck was wrong with him? "Wait a minute. Wait a minute. Don't try and pull that shit with me, that 'I'm not gay shit' because, dude, I know otherwise. You remember, I was lying there under you. I felt your dick poking against me. I know where your hands were. I know where your tongue was—in my mouth."

"Shut up!" he yelled at me. I was convinced he was going to shove me again, but he didn't. I was ready for him if he decided to do that. I also decided not to push him when he was as irrational as he was right then. I honestly thought the guy was going to cry.

"Mark," I tried again. "I'm sorry. You know I didn't plan this. I'd give anything for this not to have happened."

"Yeah, well you better fix it, you hear me?" he ordered me as he zipped up his pants and rebuckled his belt. Before I could throw some snarky comment back his way, he was out the door of my room. It sounded like he ran down the stairs and out the front door. Glancing out my bedroom window, I saw him sprinting down our long driveway toward the street.

And we did have a long driveway—way longer than it needed to be. Land wasn't as precious in the suburbs as it had been when we'd lived in the city. When my folks decided to move to the suburbs, one of the things that spoke of prosperity, of having arrived, was having a longer than necessary driveway. I didn't get it, but it was important to them. I'm sure Mark was cursing the distance he had to run to get to the street as he made his escape that Friday night, but the rat bastard had abandoned me, and that pissed me off. It also left me all alone in the house to deal with my dad. Just when I could have used the backup and support of my best friend, he'd taken off and left me to sink or swim on my own.

For maybe ten or fifteen minutes, I simply paced, thinking. Every possible scenario ran through my head about what was going to happen next. I could picture every bad scenario, but I was more challenged to come up with positive ones. I guess Mark had been right—this was bad.

It had never been my intention to tell my mom or dad that I was gay. While I was comfortable with who I was, I felt no compulsion to share that news with them or with anyone else. But that decision had been effectively removed from my list of options that night, and it left me feeling somewhat scared, powerless, and nervous.

When I paused in my thinking and walking, I realized no sound was coming from downstairs. There was always some noise, some sound, that wafted to the upstairs. The TV or some music or a ball game—something. But that night there was nothing but silence.

I needed to find out where I stood, so I took a deep breath and decided to step into the lion's den. Walking as quietly as possible, I slowly descended the stairs into the living room. The TV was off, and the room was empty. The only other place my dad might be if he was in the house was in his home office. He frequently brought work home with him and spent some time in there doing whatever it was he did.

As I stood outside his office intending to check on him, I was shocked to find the office door closed. I was almost surprised there even was a door to the room. I honestly couldn't remember the room being anything except wide open. But that night the door was closed. Had he been sitting in there with the door open, I might have had the balls to walk in and talk with him. But no fucking way was I going to open that door and go in there. No way. None.

So I got something to drink and sat down in the living room. Flipping through the hundreds of channels we got on cable, I couldn't find anything that would hold my interest. In point of fact, it would have to have been some freaking awesome program to capture my interest that night, and none of what I found even came close.

After sitting there flipping for fifteen minutes, there was still no sign of any movement from his office. The door was closed as solidly as it had been when I'd turned on the television. He had to have heard me out here. We were the only two people in the house that night. Hell, he wasn't even supposed to be there. He was supposed to be off at the country club seeing somebody or doing something. I'd thought it was the perfect time for Mark and me to finally do it. Lord knows we'd talked about it enough.

We'd had the equivalent of phone sex face-to-face more times than we could count. I don't know what you call it when you're sitting in the same room with the person fully clothed and you're telling that person what you want to do with them if they were naked. Whatever you call it, Mark and I had done it—a lot. I can say many things about my best friend Mark; he's a scrappy kid, but he's no lumbering giant. Standing just a little over five feet in height, we looked each other eye-to-eye with our socks on. Looking at his body was somewhat like looking into a mirror because we were built pretty much the same. We had all the parts other guys have, but there was nothing special about those parts. Nothing was wrong with them, but there was nothing noteworthy either. Neither of us had six-pack abs or pecs or biceps for days. Neither of us had the legs of a runner or anything like that. We were both just regular guys.

Mark was my best buddy. We'd been friends for forever. Over the years we'd grown closer and closer, spending countless hours together. We talked about everything. Well, everything except for one thing. Confessing to each other that we were gay took us a long time. It very nearly didn't happen.

Now you'd think that it would be obvious to anyone who took the trouble to look that something was different about us. Neither of us dated girls or had any interest in girls. That, alone, made us unusual, because we were at the age when testosterone was coursing through our bloodstreams, and in most guys it set off an instinctive urge to rut with a woman, or several women—hell, as many women as would have them. We were different, but somehow no one seemed to notice or care. I don't know which, but it allowed us to fly under the radar of most people, which was all either of us wanted.

When we each grew a pair of balls and told the other we were gay—I went first—everything changed. I wasn't sure what Mark was going to say when I told him. I thought I knew my best friend. I thought I knew him, but I still couldn't predict what he was going to say. Still, he was my best friend and I had to tell him, so I did.

It took him a bit longer to make the same confession to me. He told me, but he was clearly unhappy about it somehow. We kissed that night, and oh that guy can kiss. We wanted to get naked and experiment, play, do things we'd only dreamt about before. But we couldn't do that, so we kissed. We kissed and we rubbed each other, humping while we kissed in my room in the dark. We both came in our pants that night. We had to be quiet about it because my family had been home. I wanted to scream when it happened. I wanted to shout from the rooftops and give the biggest moan of pleasure any man had ever given anywhere anytime through all recorded history. It was my first time cumming with another man, and even though he hadn't touched my dick with his hands or his mouth or any part of his body, it still counted in my book, and it couldn't have been better, because my first time was with my best friend.

While Mark was clearly gay, he was also not entirely comfortable with that information. He wasn't happy he'd been born as something other than what everyone else was, especially something that, if known, would make people hate him and generally make his life miserable. So while he took every opportunity to kiss me, fondle me, and do everything he could think of with me, he clearly was conflicted. His orientation was fixed, but his happiness with that fact was not. Based on his reaction when my father caught us, clearly this issue was still in play in his mind.

My dad never did come out of his office that night. I waited for hours, convinced he would at least need to come out to pee, if nothing else. But his door remained firmly closed. I didn't look forward to my eventual conversation with him, but it needed to happen, and it clearly wasn't going to happen that night, so I went to bed.

# Chapter Two
# The Morning After

THE DAYS that followed were some of the weirdest I can remember ever experiencing. When I got up the next morning, my dad was gone—I don't know where. I asked my mother where he had gone, and she would only answer vaguely that he was "out." Clearly he'd said something to her, because she looked at me in a way she never had before. Sort of a mix between disappointed and angry and scared.

She effectively avoided me the rest of that day. I hung around the house for a while, hoping he would come back and I could talk with him. If we were going to talk, I wanted to do it and get it over with. But after a couple of hours, there was still no sign of him. Since I had nervous energy that I needed to burn off, I got on my bike and just started pedaling. I didn't have any particular destination in mind. I wasn't going anywhere to do anything. I just needed to ride, so I did. I covered miles in our mostly flat town and the surrounding suburbs.

I stopped when I felt my phone vibrate in my pocket, hoping it was a call or a text from Mark. I could handle my dad not talking to me, but it hurt to have Mark not talk to me. The text wasn't from Mark, but was instead from another friend, who told me Mark was in his living room with that friend's sister and how he'd caught them making out on the sofa just a moment before he texted me. That news was bad enough, but when a moment or two later he sent me a photo of the two of them, I was devastated. Mark's lips were supposed to be on me, on my lips, not on some random female he didn't know at all. The woman had Mark's pants undone and pushed down along with his underwear. Her hand was wrapped around his dick.

My friend's sister was known for her sexual prowess and her insatiable sexual appetite. In other words, the woman was a slut. She was the one every guy went to when they wanted a sure thing. I had nightmare visions of Mark—my Mark—getting naked with that woman and doing with her what we were supposed to do, what my father had interrupted. Hell, for all I knew, since the time that picture had been taken and texted to me, she'd gotten him out of his pants enough to get his dick inside her. I shuddered at the thought.

My world fell apart even more with this new information. Not only was my dad not speaking to me, but now Mark had gone over to the dark side, obviously in some desperate move to prove to the world that he wasn't gay, all because he was afraid my dad was going to call his dad and tell him. How he could bury his true nature deeply enough to do what that picture showed him doing was beyond me.

For days I tried to reach Mark to ask him that very question. I texted him, I called him. I left messages on his Facebook account. I was practically ready to send smoke signals, but he ignored me no matter how I tried to reach him. Several times I got on my bike and rode over to his house, knocking and ringing the bell. No one ever came to the door, regardless of the hour at which I went to visit. I knew for a fact that someone was home at least once.

On about my fifth visit to his house, I knocked and rang the bell as usual and waited before doing it again. I was just turning to leave when the front door unexpectedly swung open and Mark was suddenly in my face. At least it was someone who looked vaguely like my Mark. This Mark was angry. His beautiful face was curled up into a hateful, angry sneer.

"What the fuck do you want?" he demanded of me with more harshness than I'd ever heard in his voice before.

"I just wanted to see if you were okay." Surely he couldn't find that objectionable. Ha.

"I want you to leave me alone. I'm no goddamned faggot like you are. If you keep stalking me, I will—"

"Wait a minute, wait a minute," I interrupted him. "First of all, if I'm a faggot, as you just called me, then, buddy boy, you are too, because you and I were the only ones there in that room on that bed. You and me. Nobody else. And I was the one on his back with you on top of me, holding me down and humping against my body. So cut the crap and stop using the word faggot—I hate that word, and you should too."

"Leave me alone," Mark said through obviously gritted teeth. "You can be or do anything you want, but don't be dragging me into that shit. I don't care what you do, but keep your hands off me."

"A little bit of revisionist history going on here, my friend."

"Shut the fuck up and get off our property before I call the cops."

"Mark," I tried one last time, "it's me. I'm not the enemy. Please talk to me. What the hell is going on with you? Are you really that scared? Why?" For a moment I thought I was getting through to him. For a split second or two, I thought I saw the Mark I knew present with me, but he didn't hang around long enough to do much good.

Before I knew it was happening, my former best friend hauled back his right arm and slugged me in the face. He hit me hard enough that I went backward and fell down the stairs leading up to his front porch. I was stunned. Mark—at least the Mark I knew or thought I knew—would never have done something like that. My Mark was gentle and peaceful. He was a pacifist who hated violence. The guy who had just hit me? Well, I honestly had no idea who he was. All I knew was I didn't like this Mark. The Mark I knew wouldn't have been such a coward. I didn't know this Mark, didn't like him, and didn't want to stick around. Turned out not to be a choice I had anyway, because Mark went back into his house and slammed the door closed behind him.

# Chapter Three
# Losing My Best Friend

USUALLY WHEN something happened that was important, Mark was the first person I called and shared it with. But now that Mark had been beamed up by the space aliens and replaced by some creature I didn't recognize, I didn't have that option any longer. I didn't have a fallback guy to go to, even though now I really needed one.

So I had to try to figure out what to do all on my own with no one to bounce ideas off of. My dad wasn't talking to me—I guess that was actually a good thing. Mark wasn't talking to me—I guess that was also a good thing since I didn't recognize him anymore and couldn't communicate with him even if he was talking with me.

With no other choices, I spent a lot of time alone over the following couple of days. I would rather have had someone to talk with. Hell, who wouldn't? Especially now when I was so confused about everything, but I didn't have that person and I didn't know how to go about finding that person on the fly. Little did I know, though, that my list of problems was only just beginning and was soon about to make a major leap forward into whole new territory.

Three days after he'd unexpectedly entered my bedroom at the world's worst possible moment, my dad paid me a repeat visit. The only problem was that this visit was no more welcome that his last had been.

With no preliminaries, he just walked in and issued an order. "Pack a bag. We're going on a trip."

"Huh?"

He didn't repeat his instructions but simply stood and looked at me.

"Where are we going?" I asked when he didn't share anything further with me.

"Pack whatever you'll need for several weeks." Without another word he turned and left. I didn't know what the hell he was talking about, so I got off my bed and followed him downstairs.

"What are you talking about? What trip? Where?"

"Simple. Pack."

"For what? Where are we going?"

"Away. Get packed."

"When?" I tried to get some more information.

I should have figured the answer wasn't going to be to my liking when he looked at his watch. "About twenty minutes. You better get going."

I pushed, I prodded, I yelled. I tried a bunch of things, but none of them worked at getting him to share any more details with me, so I finally just gave up and went upstairs. I thought about ignoring him and seeing what happened, but I bagged that idea and reluctantly grabbed a couple of bags and started throwing some stuff into them. It really was hard to pack for a trip when you didn't know where you were going, how you were going to get there, and how long you were going to be gone.

Before I was ready—if I could ever be ready—he reappeared in my bedroom doorway and asked, "You ready to go?"

"No," I answered with my best belligerent attitude. My best pissed-off tone didn't seem to do much good, though.

"Get your bags in the car in five minutes." I was getting pretty fed up with him and his orders like that. The least he could do was tell me something about what was up. All I knew was that I probably wasn't going to like whatever he had in mind. But again he was gone before I could voice my objections.

With no alternative that I could identify, five minutes later I was walking out the front door of our house, hauling my two bags full of my shit—or at least what I could shove into those bags. My dad was already standing beside the car.

"Dad, talk to me. Where are we going?"

"Put your bags in the car and let's get going." I hated being ignored, and he was doing a major job of ignoring me that morning.

Before I could ask him or push him some more, he got into the car and was sitting behind the wheel. I knew he couldn't hear me even if I tried yelling at him because he had the engine running and the windows closed. I wasn't sure if he would leave without me—probably not—but I was tempted to give it a shot. But I didn't want to further irritate him, so I tossed my two bags in the back end of the car and got into the front passenger seat. Before I even had my seat belt fastened, he had the car in reverse and we were backing out of the driveway.

For the next few minutes I paid careful attention to where we were headed, since I had absolutely no clue. For all I knew, he was taking me to some military school or some equally horrible thing. I wanted to ask, but I knew he would only ignore me, so I didn't even bother. I just slumped down in my seat and stewed. Every once in a while, I glared toward my father, but he remained a solid stone wall—unbending, unmoving, unbreakable—so I didn't even bother trying because I knew all it would do was piss me off further, and I already felt majorly pissed off with him. He stared forward, and I stared down, occasionally glaring at him. We were at a standoff.

I wanted to scream, to rant, to stomp my feet, to protest his entire approach to his learning that I was not exactly who he'd always assumed I was. I wanted to talk with him about it. Sure, I hadn't planned to tell him right now, nor in the way in which he'd actually learned about it, but it was what it was. He knew now, and he'd found out in not the best possible way. I couldn't change that and neither could he, no matter how much we both might want to do so.

By watching the direction in which he drove, I was able to rule out some things. For example, we were headed north, so I knew we were not headed for New York City. Yeah, right, fat chance of that. The idea of him dumping me at some military academy was looking frighteningly more possible since we were headed north, and I knew there were places like that scattered all around New England.

At the two-hour point, still without a single word from my father, I really wanted to stop to pee. Who knew how long we still had to go to get to where we were headed. I didn't know if we had ten minutes left to go or if we still had hours and hours of driving ahead of us. I decided to wait. Eventually we'd have to at least stop to buy gas for the car.

He probably was thinking of his behavior as being the strong and silent type, but I saw him more as a guy with a big stick up his butt. So I sat there growing more and more uncomfortable with each passing mile. My bladder needed to relieve some pressure. I was finally about to tell him this, when completely out of the blue he steered the car off the highway into a small middle-of-nowhere place.

He pulled off the secondary road into some gas station-cum-convenience store-cum-fast-food restaurant. In other words, the roadside stop was a multiple purpose facility, a one-stop shop for all of your highway needs.

"Are we there yet?" I asked.

"Bathroom break," he answered, using the absolute minimum number of words necessary. I wasn't going to use the bathroom at the same time he did, so I poked around in the convenience store part of the place, making a mental list of a couple of things I could pick up if we still had a long ways to go yet.

We made the switch with me taking my turn in the bathroom. When I came back out, I saw my dad was still inside talking to the kid behind the counter. I moved closer to listen a little, hoping that I might finally get some insight into where we were going. No such luck.

"Thank you," I heard him say to the kid just as I got within earshot.

"Are we there yet?" I decided to ask again, even though I already knew the answer to the question.

The kid behind the counter wasn't helping by just smiling in our direction.

"Nope," he answered.

I was tired of this game. "How much farther do we have to go? Should I buy something to eat while we're here?"

He probably wouldn't have answered me if all I'd said was the first part, but the second part caught his attention. "Couldn't hurt," he told me as he turned and walked up and down the aisles quickly to pick up something of his own. I already knew what I wanted so by the time he'd made his selection I already had mine at the counter, waiting for him to hopefully pay for both—it worked and he did.

Back in the car, he was as chatty as he had been during the first couple of hours. With nothing but fields to look at, I was bored out of my gourd. Mile after monotonous mile we hurried on down the road to some undisclosed location. I had no clue if it was for a day, a week, a month, or forever. I hated feeling so not in control.

Probably about an hour after we had left the convenience store, the silence was broken.

"I know you're curious about where we're going."

I grunted, refusing to speak, which I know was a bit counterproductive given the long silence we'd endured. I wasn't going to stand in the way of him speaking.

"Do you remember that I inherited an old farm in upstate?"

"No," I told him, because I didn't. "What farm?"

"Well, I did. My father inherited it from his grandfather, but my father hated country life and wanted nothing to do with country living. He rented it out or did something with it. When he died it passed to me."

"Why've I never heard about this?"

"Probably because it's never been relevant before."

"And why is it now?" I asked.

"It's relevant now because that's where we're going. You and I are going to live there."

"Why?" I demanded. "You're no more a farmer than your dad was."

"I needed to get you away from the city. It was corrupting you. It was making things too easy for you."

My mouth hung open. His words were like a slap across my face. I was stunned.

"What the hell are you talking about?" I asked him loudly.

"I saw you and that boy… that night… on your bed."

"Yeah, so?"

"So? Jesus, Adam. Listen to yourself. No one in our family has ever been one of those people, and we're not going to start now. I had to get you away from temptation, so that's what I'm doing. We're going to live on the farm."

"What about Mom?" I don't know why I asked this, since she was gone more than she was around, always off in Europe or somewhere. We went months at a time without seeing her.

"She's busy."

"Are you two breaking up? Is that what this is all about?"

"No."

"I've got friends back there. We're going back before the school year starts, right? I'm about to be a senior in high school. I'm going to graduate from high school!"

"You and I are here for the indefinite future."

"Dad!"

"Don't argue with me," he yelled. "Someday you'll thank me for doing this. For saving you."

"Dad!" This was just too fucked-up for words. I had heard all the words, but my mind was reeling with confusion. All of this crap was flying at me from out of nowhere. What the fuck was I going to do? I didn't know squat about living in the country, and neither did he. I didn't see how he could sit there and tell me he was saving me and then rip me away from everything I knew—my home, my friends, hell, even my family. What was he thinking?

It only took one look at how rigidly he was sitting in the driver's seat and to see the look of fierce determination on his face to know that I wasn't going to get anything out of him. I wanted to scream, to throw something, to rant, but I fought back those urges and slumped back into my seat.

# Chapter Four
# On the Road Again

TWENTY MINUTES passed with nothing but the sound of car tires rhythmically running over the highway surface. My dad used the GPS device that was part of his car to guide us to our destination. Even though I hated to show interest, I kept glancing at the thing every time it gave some new bit of information or some fresh instruction, such as "Turn left in 500 yards." I perked up as we did as the GPS instructed and left the highway at Exit 8.

The view out the window was—what? I guess the best way to describe it was green. Everything was green—lush and green. Green leaves, green bushes, green shrubs. Green everywhere. It looked like we'd exited from the highway into the middle of nowhere. There were no houses visible, no town, no nothing other than green.

My dad followed instructions and steered to the right and down a long hill. When the road dead-ended, I was able to see the beginnings of at least some activity, some sign of life, of civilization. There were a couple of houses, a church, and off to our left lay the hope for more buildings.

A left hand turn at the intersection took us through what I guess could be called a settled area. Things were spaced out, so nothing was next to anything else. As a suburban dweller my entire life, I wasn't used to seeing so much open space. It felt wrong.

Looking to the right, my dad pointed to something and announced, "I guess that's the local grocery store." I followed his direction and saw something that was tiny compared to the stores we had back home.

"My God," he said, "they're even here." It took me a minute to figure out that he was talking about McDonald's. There was yet another of those multiple purpose roadside stores with convenience items, fast food, and gas. My father was no fan of McDonald's. I'd never bothered to ask him why, and at that moment I just didn't care.

I was surprised when he turned the car off the road and then did a big U-turn. I quickly glanced, hoping that nothing was coming. He must have seen my glance because he told me, "Don't worry. There's a lot less traffic out here than in the city."

As if our first view of the "town" wasn't enough, we drove back through the single strip of settlement. We crossed a bridge and then turned left and crossed another bridge. Another left took us up one mother-big hill. I couldn't remember ever seeing a hill so steep as this one. I supposed it wasn't all that big, but it sure felt it as we started going up. At the summit of the hill we turned right onto a primitive-looking dirt road. Where the fuck was he taking me?

It felt like the very top of the world—a world filled with green. We were surrounded by fields of green, something that looked like big grass.

"Look at that corn," he said, tipping his head toward the left.

"Is that corn?" I was a city boy. I didn't know these things.

"Yes, that's corn. I remember my grandfather saying that the corn had to be knee high by the Fourth of July. It looks like that shouldn't be a problem this year. Everything looks all green and lush. Farmers must be really happy."

"Are you planning to become a farmer?" I asked, trying to not laugh at the idea of my father being a farmer. My dad was many things, but I had a very hard time picturing him as a country boy or a farmer.

"No, I'm not—but you are."

"Huh?" What the fuck was he talking about now?

"I said you are. You're going to work on a farm."

"Why the fuck would I want to do that?" I demanded.

"Because that's what you're going to do."

"No."

"Yes. It's all set up. This afternoon we're going to get settled, and I'm going to take you over to where you'll be working."

"No."

"Don't argue with me, Adam. You're doing it."

"Why? What the hell is…? Why are you doing this? Why are you torturing me? So I'm gay—so what? I like guys, not girls. What's the big deal? Lots of folks are gay, Dad."

"Not you. You're not gay. You will not be gay. You're my only son. If we want to continue our family line, you need to marry and have children. You need a son to pass everything on to when that time comes."

"Dad! What the hell are you talking about? Children? Dad! I'm seventeen."

"It's what seventeen-year-old guys do. It's what they think about all the time. When I was seventeen, my buddies and I were all constantly plotting how we could get into the pants on any of a half dozen different girls. It's what guys do and have done forever."

"Not all guys, Dad. Girls don't do it for me. I'm sorry, but it's not gonna happen."

"You can't know until you've dated a few girls and slept with some of them. Trust me."

"That is so not going to happen," I told him. This day just kept getting more and more crazy.

I was so outraged by what I was hearing that I hadn't realized we'd stopped. We were no longer moving. In other words, we'd parked. I looked off to my right and saw—yep, you guessed it—more green. Straight ahead of us, though, was an old farmhouse. I guess you could call it "rustic." Or else you could call it broken down and in serious need of repair. The place was big, but it really had seen better days.

"Why'd we stop?" I asked him.

"We're here."

"This? You're kidding, right?"

"This is the house. All of this land is mine… and someday it will be yours… and then someday you'll pass it on to your son."

"Yeah, whatever," I muttered as I got out of the car.

"This place better have cable," I told him, fearing the worst. He was already climbing the rickety-looking stairs to the front porch. I wondered how he was going to get in without a key, but the solution was easier than I'd realized—the door wasn't locked.

I followed him into the house and looked around. All I could see was dust, dirt, and something that I guess had at one time been white sheets lying across what must have been the furniture. Clearly no one lived there, and no one had lived there in a very long time.

"This place is disgusting," I told him, reluctant to touch anything.

He led me into the kitchen—at least I think it was the kitchen. If the house looked old, the kitchen was just plain ancient. The stove was huge. "Where are the knobs?" I asked.

"What?"

"The stove," I gestured. "There's no buttons or knobs. How the hell do you turn on the heat to cook?"

"We'll figure that out."

Since I was by the sink, I turned on the water faucets. Usually when you do that, water comes out. In this house, all I got was the sound of something rattling and shaking, accompanied by a gurgling sound I'd never heard before. Finally, something splatted out of the faucet into the sink. It happened too fast for me to be able to tell if it was water or not. A few seconds later something more came out—this time more and a bit longer.

"No," I told Dad as I watched brown, disgusting water come out of the faucet. There was a small flow now, a trickle, all of it brown. "Dad! Look at that! We can't live here."

"Of course we can. We're men. We're tough."

"Dad, we're *city* men, not country men. Do you know how to fix that?" I asked, gesturing angrily with my hand at the faucet running a small trickle of brown water. "Huh?"

"We'll get it all sorted out."

"Oh, yeah, sure. You betcha."

I watched as he pulled open the door of an ancient refrigerator. The thing looked huge from the outside, but inside it looked really small. "Do you see a cord?" he asked as he looked on the left side.

"Yeah, I guess," I told him, squeezing down to pick up the end of an old electrical cord.

"Plug it in," he ordered. "We'll let that cool off. Okay, here's what we're going to do. You're going to get to work cleaning this place up."

"You're kidding, right?"

"Adam, stop fighting me on this. It's a done deal. Get over all this complaining crap. It's not doing you a bit of good."

"Why didn't I get any say in this? Huh? It's my life you're ruining. Why didn't you ask me?"

"Adam, I'm your father. I'm responsible for you and your well-being. It's my job to raise you and prepare you for life in the real world. It's my job to make a man out of you. You're on that great divide between being a boy and being a man. It's a father's job to teach his son how to be a man. I realize that I've not been a very good father to you. I've been more focused on work and earning a living than I have been on my family. Your sister has your mother, but you are my responsibility. I'm the only one who can teach you what you need to know to jump that divide and become a man.

"You've given me a wake-up call. Adam, I'm sorry I've let you down and not been there for you, to teach you, to answer your questions—"

"Dad, what are you talking about? You've been great. You always have been."

"No," he told me so matter-of-factly I was speechless. "No, I haven't. If I had done my job, I never would have found you doing what... what I saw you doing. It's my fault, but I'm not giving up. We've lost a lot of time, but we're going to give you a crash course in manhood."

I was so flabbergasted that I wanted to fall into a chair. The only problem was that everything in sight was disgusting, and the thought of touching it was enough to make my skin crawl.

"Okay, you get to work cleaning, and I'm going to go back into town for a supply run. We need food, we need... well, we need everything. I'll be back."

I wanted to scream, to rant, but he was gone before I could do anything. As I heard the car start, I wondered if he was going to leave me and just never come back. I was so far from anything, from everything I knew, that I had no clue how I would ever get back home from here. Was that his plan? Who knew? Nothing he'd said in the last twenty minutes made the slightest bit of sense to me.

My bags were still in the back end of the car, but I at least had my backpack with the most essential things. I kept my backpack firmly hooked over my shoulders so I didn't have to set it down onto anything that hadn't been cleaned off yet.

Suddenly I was alone in a strange place. My eyes told me that the house was filthy, and my nose verified that finding. I sneezed from stirring up just a bit of dust. I didn't want to sit down or touch anything, so I went out of the house and just walked all the way around, half hoping I'd find something different on the other side. From the outside it looked big and old. When I walked back inside and explored a little bit, it looked the same—big and old.

Everywhere I walked the floors creaked, and the house made sounds that didn't make me feel all warm and fuzzy. The condition of everything was appalling. The house was beyond filthy. How in the world we were supposed to live here was beyond me.

After wandering around the house for about twenty minutes, I found an ancient vacuum cleaner. But when I plugged it in and tried to turn it on, I made a big discovery—it didn't work. Spying a light switch on the wall, or at least what I took to be a light switch, I tried pushing the buttons to turn on the lights and learned the reason the cleaner didn't work was the same reason the lights didn't turn on—the house had no power.

# Chapter Five
# A Lack of Power

ABOUT AN hour after he'd left, I heard a car. Pushing the broken-down screen door open, I moved out the front door and descended the three front steps.

"Why aren't you inside cleaning?" he demanded.

"Couldn't. No power. No broom."

"What? The power was supposed to be turned on yesterday."

"No power. No cleaning. No refrigerator. No nothing. We can't stay here."

"Son of a bitch." He was quiet for a moment. "Come on," he ordered as he got back into the car.

I joined him and asked, "Where are we going?"

"Neighbor." He didn't offer any further explanation as he drove back to the dirt road in front of the farmhouse and turned left to proceed down the road farther than we had before. It was only about a mile, so we were there very quickly. The house we went to was nearly identical to the one we'd just left, only this one was in better shape, better cared for—and it looked lived in, not abandoned like the house we'd just left.

Bounding up the stairs, my dad pounded on the door and called out, "Melinda? Melinda? You here?"

A moment later the screen door was pushed open and a handsome but slightly weathered woman stepped out, giving him a big smile.

"Dennis?"

"Yes. Good to finally meet you face-to-face. This is my son Adam." I waved in her direction and said, "Hey."

"We've got a problem. There's no power at the house."

"What? They were supposed to get that turned on yesterday. Come on in. I'll call them right now."

"I just went to the store and bought a whole bunch of stuff that needs to be kept cold, but we don't have a refrigerator. Is there any chance you might have some room to hold things for a day or two until we get this sorted out?"

"Of course. Bring it on in here," she told him. My dad turned to me and made some kind of gesture toward the car, which I took to mean that he wanted me to retrieve his purchases and haul them inside.

My dad and Melinda had disappeared into the house somewhere, so I pulled the front door open and walked in, intending to follow them to wherever they had gone. But before I had even taken six steps, I came to a complete halt when I heard an angry male voice demand, "Who the hell are you?" It took me a moment, but I found the source of the voice—one of the most stunningly gorgeous men I think I had ever seen. Except for the obvious anger that rolled off him, the guy was hotter than hot. But the anger was a pretty big issue.

He quickly descended the stairs and stood in front of me. "I asked you a question." Shoving his finger into my chest and pushing me back, he repeated, a little louder this time, "Who the hell are you? What makes you think you can just walk in here? You planning to rob us?"

My hands were full, so I couldn't offer to shake his hand. "I'm Adam. Who are you?"

"You make a habit of just walking into people's houses uninvited?"

"What? No. My dad's with some woman who I think lives here."

All the time I was trying to explain to this crazy guy what was going on, he kept backing me up by continuing to herd me toward the wall.

"Ben!"

Had I not been staring at him, I wouldn't have believed it, but at the sound of that one tiny word, the guy who'd been getting awfully aggressive with me actually jumped and transformed from frightening into frightened—almost. The voice startled him, and I had seen it happen.

"What?" the guy, whose name was apparently Ben, asked with a certain belligerence that clearly was not well received by the woman I'd seen my dad with a moment earlier.

"You behave yourself, mister. I didn't raise you to show such bad manners. Now you apologize to Adam and then say hello."

Clearly apologizing was not something he wanted to do, and I wasn't sure if it was the idea or if it was apologizing to me. I was going with the idea that he didn't want to do it because he had no clue who I was—or so I thought. It turned out I was already a known concept and that I was the last one to figure this out.

"Yeah, whatever," Ben said.

"Benjamin!" his mother scolded him.

"Sorry," he muttered, and it was completely unclear if he was apologizing to her or to me, which was probably just fine as far as he was concerned. Without another word he brushed past me and was gone a few seconds later. From my point of view, this was no great loss.

Ben might have been reluctant to own up to his behavior, but his mother was not. "I'm so sorry. He's a good boy. He's just been under a lot more pressure since his dad died. It hasn't been that long, and Ben really misses him. He's been short with everybody."

"I'm sorry to hear about your loss," I told her, not knowing what else to say.

"Thank you. It caught all of us by surprise. Ben's taken it hard. He and his dad were close."

"What happened?" I asked, which probably wasn't a reasonable question to ask.

"Heart attack. It happened out in the fields one day. Ben found him when he didn't come in when we expected him. I think he's blaming himself."

"For a heart attack? That doesn't make any sense."

"Thank you," she agreed. "But once that boy gets an idea in his head, he can be as stubborn as a mule."

She took one of the bags I was still holding and guided me into one of the biggest kitchens I think I've ever seen. I mean, the room was massive. Finding some place to store all of the groceries my dad had bought was not a problem. There were two big refrigerators, not to mention a separate freezer. I was in awe. I had never seen a home that had need for so much cold storage.

"Have you boys eaten?" she asked. I looked around, wondering who the other "boy" she was referring to was. When my dad answered, I figured it must be him. I didn't think of him in those terms, but if she wanted to, who was I to stop her?

"I made something that I was going to bring over to you this evening, but since you're here, you can have it now if you'd like."

"Food would be good," I volunteered since I was hungry.

Melinda pointed me toward plates and silverware and put me to work setting a table in the kitchen while she busied herself with something I couldn't see. Since there were four chairs at the table, I set four places, hoping against hope that the surly one named Ben was not going to join us. That hope was dashed, though, when Melinda called him to the table before we sat down.

The expression on his face when he spotted me as he entered the room told me all I needed to know—Ben was not happy.

"What's he still doing here?" he asked his mother.

"Benjamin Francis Taylor! I did not raise you to behave so rudely. We have guests. You behave yourself, or you and I will have words later. Do you understand me?"

"Yes ma'am," he answered reluctantly.

"Now, say hello to our neighbors. This is Dennis," she told him, introducing my father, "and his son, Adam." He shook my dad's hand but only grunted at me. I really didn't understand what I'd done to piss him off so much.

The four of us sat at the table and ate a wonderful dinner. Melinda certainly knew how to cook—of that there was no question. She and my dad talked, but Ben and I were largely silent. I took advantage of the opportunity to get a better look at Ben. I'd been so distracted earlier by his anger that I hadn't had a chance to truly absorb how hot he was—Ben was a hunk.

His hair was a dirty blond as near as I could tell. The only reason it was difficult to be sure was that he kept it cut very short, so there wasn't a lot of hair to look at to gather data. His face was beautifully structured in a classic V shape. He was probably easily six feet in height. While he was muscular, he was not some hyperpumped, muscle-bound creature, which was good, because I found that type to be overdone and more annoying than anything else.

While we ate, I continued my inventory of Ben for lack of anything else to do. His hands intrigued me. Ben had long fingers, not at all roughened by physical labor. I'm sure he was accustomed to physical labor if he was a farmer, but his hands did not reveal a lifetime of labor. If anything, his hands were almost delicate in appearance. His long fingers were carefully cleaned, his nails perfectly trimmed and maintained.

I couldn't see his eyes to see what they looked like when they were not filled with distrust, but, as near as I could tell from earlier, they were a sharp shade of gray. I couldn't recall ever seeing anyone with gray eyes before, but there was no question that that was the color of Ben's eyes—at least his eyes when angry. Presumably they didn't change color when he was calm or happy, assuming he ever got into such a mood.

My study of Ben was interrupted when my father brought up something that chilled me.

"So, Adam, Melinda and Ben are in need of help here on their farm."

"Yeah. So?" I asked.

Melinda chimed in. "It's just Ben and me. Poor Ben's been doing the bulk of the heavy lifting. I couldn't do it without him. But we can't afford to hire any help."

"Well, you've got some extra help now," he told her, "and free on top of that." Where the hell was he going with this?

"Free? Who works for free?"

"Adam."

"Excuse me?" I asked, not liking the direction this conversation was taking.

"Adam has his entire summer ahead of him and nothing to do other than clean out our house and make it habitable."

"Benjamin! You were supposed to do that," Melinda scolded her son.

"I have a farm to run. I'm not some frigging maid."

She sighed. "I'm sorry. He was supposed to get that done for you. But he's right that he's been running pretty much nonstop seven days a week trying to keep up around here since Robbie passed."

"So it does sound like you could use some help. Adam would be glad to help out. No cost."

"What?" I demanded angrily. "I don't know anything about farm work."

Ben chimed in to the conversation again. "I don't have time to babysit some soft city boy spending his summer in the country."

"Ben," my dad said, "we're here until Adam finishes high school in a year."

"We are what?" I demanded.

"We are."

"Fuck that shit," I swore.

Now it was his turn to be unhappy with his offspring—me. "Adam! Language, young man." Rather than look at him for fear I'd swear more, I looked away, which happened to be toward where Ben was sitting, and I caught him almost smiling. When he saw me looking his way, the smile vanished quickly, but still I'd caught sight of it for long enough to know that it was real and that it was there.

The main course was topped off with some of the best apple pie I think I've ever tasted. I made sure to tell Melinda this. She served it with a great big hunk of cheese, which practically melted in my mouth—I think I actually moaned at the taste of it.

"Good stuff, isn't it?" my dad asked. "Melinda is noted for the cheese she makes."

"You… make this? How do you *make* cheese? I thought you bought cheese in a store."

"Where do you think they get it, Einstein?" Ben asked snarkily.

I was coming to despise Ben.

"How the hell should I know? Why the hell would I care?"

Taking a space between the two of us, Melinda told me, "Well, Adam, by the end of the summer, you'll have a better understanding of how it all happens."

Continuing to ignore me, my dad told her, "Whatever you need, Melinda. Like we talked about on the telephone, Adam is available to help, and I want you to put him to work. This summer is my opportunity to make a man out of him."

I muttered something that probably wasn't fit for civilized company, so I was just as glad no one could hear the actual words I used.

"Like I told you on the phone, we can always use help. Farming is a labor-intensive operation. I handle the cheese-making part of the operation and run our farm stand. During the summer we're open seven days a week. If you're serious, Dennis, and if Adam doesn't object—"

"He doesn't," my dad volunteered without even looking at me. Was he deliberately trying to piss me off? Because if he was, he was doing a crackerjack job at it, and if he wasn't trying to piss me off, then he was just plain sadistic, and I didn't want to spend any more time with him than absolutely necessary. The only thing that I could say for sure was that Ben was taking entirely too much pleasure in my dilemma. His bad attitude had transformed into joy at my discomfort.

"Yeah, Ma, I'll put him to work. I suspect he'll work like he's never worked before." He snickered and I sneered.

"Good," he told Ben. "Make him work. Show him how real men work for a living." Okay, it was hard to believe, but I was even more pissed off with him now—majorly pissed off. "Thanks for such a wonderful dinner, Melinda. Now, since you worked so hard, Adam will clean up."

"Ben'll help," she immediately volunteered.

"I've got work to do," Ben complained. One thing I had to give Ben was that he had a very expressive face. My guess was that he thought he didn't, but he really did. Maybe he played poker. If he played poorly I could maybe clean up. Time would tell.

"Ben, for once in your life would you please just do what I asked you to do?" his mother complained. He sighed at her, growled at me, and started hauling dishes from the table to the sink. Since he was hauling, I decided to start washing. I didn't know where anything was stored so I figured that was the best use of my time.

Most likely just to be contrary, Ben told me, "Maybe I wanted to wash." I know I shouldn't have done it, but I'd had enough of his bad attitude. It was one thing if I'd earned it, but I hadn't done anything to him to earn this treatment. What did I do? I took the dishcloth that was sopping wet with soapy hot water and I tossed it to him. "Okay, so wash," I told him while the cloth was in midair. He didn't expect me to do that, so his T-shirt got soaked. His mother laughed, which profoundly did not help my position one iota, but for a brief shining moment I felt better about how my "relationship" with Ben was falling out.

"I'll get you for that," he snarled at me quietly.

"Whatever your problem is, I wish you'd get over it. I don't know you or why you're being so miserable to me. I've never met you before today, so I know it's nothing I've done. Whatever bug is up your butt, I really wish you'd grow up and get over it. You gonna wash or do you want me to keep going?"

The dishcloth came flying back at me. I caught it in midair, something Ben hadn't done. I'd played baseball in earlier years, and one thing I'd always been able to do was to catch really well, so it was no big deal for me. Also, Ben's shirt had absorbed a lot of the water that had been in the cloth at one time so it didn't have as much water to do damage with. Without another word of commentary I got back to work washing the dinner dishes. Ben didn't stick around but went out the back door.

When Melinda reappeared, I had just one question for her. "What did I do wrong? Or is your son always in such a miserable mood?"

She sighed. "Today was especially bad for him because we had to put his favorite horse down. She was old and... well, it was time. Ben loved that horse and had had her for years. I'm afraid he's hurting more than usual tonight, and you just happened to be an easy target."

"I'm sorry to hear about his horse."

"We don't need the horses anymore, but we kept them because Ben loves them so much and simply couldn't stand the thought of getting rid of them. And he's just plain overtired. He's trying to do too much, and I haven't had any choice because it's just the two of us. When your father called and said he was looking for something for you to do, I practically leaped at his offer.

"Ben told me he's quitting school so he can work the farm full-time."

"That's stupid," I told her. "Sorry. It's just that graduating first will open so many more doors for him later in life."

"I know that and you know that, but try telling him that." She left the room, which left me alone in the big kitchen. In short order I had the dishes washed, dried, and stacked to one side since I didn't have a clue where they lived when not in use. I wiped down the counters and the table, and then I went off to find where everybody had gone.

"Adam, Melinda suggested that we spend the night here since we can't do anything over at our house. She called the power company and we're on their schedule for first thing in the morning. You and I can spend tomorrow getting started cleaning and getting settled and then you can come help Melinda and Ben."

"I don't think Ben wants my help."

"Nonsense—he needs help and you've got lots of time to help him out."

"I really don't think he wants me anywhere near him."

"Tough. You two just need to work it out, whatever it is."

Rather than continuing to argue a losing battle, I grabbed a bag from the car, went to the guest bedroom to which Melinda directed me, and changed into a pair of loose shorts and a sleeveless T-shirt. It had gotten quite hot that day, and the old farmhouse was not air-conditioned. After sweating over the hot sink I couldn't wait to get into something more comfortable.

I lay on the bed with the door open for cross ventilation and spent some time reading. I saw Ben pass by several times. It seemed like he was spending an inordinate amount of time studying something about the room I was in, but I did my level best to ignore him. After about the sixth time he slowly passed the door to my room I asked, "Something I can help you with, Ben?" I was determined to be as pleasant as I could possibly be.

"What?" he asked, his voice sounding like he thought he'd been slick and he was now surprised he'd been caught doing something he shouldn't have been doing.

"I said is there something I can help you with?"

"Nope. Why?"

"You kept looking in like you wanted to ask me something."

He was silent for a moment, as if thinking. "Maybe I was wondering what you did to piss off your dad."

"Why do you think I did something to piss him off?"

"You're here—that's why."

"I'm sorry about your horse. That must… it must have been hard, and it must have hurt. I'm sorry you've had to go through that today." I decided to try a different approach with him.

Ben's eyes went wide with surprise, and what I think was a hint of the hurt he was likely feeling.

"She was really old," he told me.

# Chapter Six
# Getting Up with the Chickens

AS A child of the urban jungle, I was not accustomed to living without the creature comforts, like air-conditioning. It was hot that night, maybe not more than other days around then, but it was very hot for me. I hadn't tried sleeping without air-conditioning in years, so that first night in the guest bedroom of the neighbor's farmhouse was tough.

I didn't want to sleep with the bedroom door open because I didn't usually wear anything to bed, and I couldn't have either of the strangers wandering past the open door with me hanging out for everyone to see. But it was so beastly hot with the door closed that I had to pull on some shorts and open the door back up in the hopes of getting some sort of a breeze.

I can't call that night my most restful night ever. It might have been better or easier if some idiot hadn't started to make all kinds of noise throughout the house at some unbelievably early hour of the morning. In other words, just when the night cooled off enough to be able to get some decent sleep, someone was up and seemed determined that everyone else in the house was going to be up too.

When it was clear that it wasn't just a mistake, I cracked one eye open to look at my watch. *Who the freaking hell gets up at 4:45 a.m.?* That's what I wanted to know. I could not imagine why anyone would need to be up at such a ridiculous hour. Didn't farmers sort of need the sunlight to be able to do... well, anything?

Fumbling around in the dark for my T-shirt and shorts so I could go investigate, I finally figured out that I was already wearing them.

I didn't have any trouble finding the person or people who were up that morning because they had lights on everywhere—yet another reason they should wait until the big light in the sky was turned on before getting up. I stumbled into the kitchen to find Ben and his mother both up, and both acting entirely too perky. My eyes were only half open.

"Did Canada invade or something? Do we all have to go fight? Is that why you're both up before the light? I don't fight well before I've had coffee."

Ben laughed and I very nearly fell for it.

"I give it a week," he said, laughing as he left the house.

Looking at his mother through my half-opened eyes, I said something wise like, "Huh?"

"You're not a morning person, are you?" she asked.

"Ask me again when we get to the morning."

"Oh, darling, for farmers it is morning. We have more work than could possibly be done during just the daylight hours." My brain heard the words but was a little sluggish processing them. Things improved when she shoved a cup of coffee in my hands. The smell was heavenly. Ah, that heady aroma. Nectar of the gods in a mug. It was as good as it smelled. While I communed with my coffee, Melinda fixed breakfast for me. Breakfast was as hearty as the dinner the previous evening had been—hearty and incredibly tasty. Melinda was an awesome cook. My mother was an okay cook, which was partly why I helped out with the cooking at home. The thought of "home," though, soured the good work the coffee had done.

She was looking out the window over the sink while holding her own cup of coffee, studying something. "The power company just got to your house. We should go over there."

"Good luck getting my dad out of bed at this hour."

"I'm not even going to try. You can if you want. What do you say you and I drive over there and get to work?"

"If you say so, sure, I guess. You haven't seen the place. It's a disgusting mess."

"I'm not surprised. No one has lived there in years. I'm sorry Ben didn't get started on the cleaning like I said he would."

BY THE time my dad appeared in our house, Melinda and I had been hard at work for hours. We were both caked in dust and dirt and grime, but at least there were some visible signs of progress. It was a good thing Melinda had brought her vacuum cleaner along on our little venture because the vacuum that came with the house was so frigging heavy it would take a team of six people to lift the thing up and down the stairs. I used the house vacuum on the main floor while Melinda worked upstairs.

With power restored, the refrigerator was running. The refrigerator at home was nearly silent as it went about its assigned task. Not so the refrigerator that sat in the kitchen of this house. It made so much noise that it sounded like someone was kicking down the back door each time it cycled off. On top of that, the thing didn't put out enough cold air to do much good at all. After running for nearly four hours it was difficult to tell that it was doing much good at all. Clearly, if we were going to be staying here, he was going to have to spring for some new appliances.

One additional benefit of having power was that the water pump was now working, so when we turned on one of the faucets, we had a good flow of water, and it was mostly clear after the lines were flushed. So having power was a good thing. Not having air conditioning was not such a good thing. After half a day of hard work in dirty, disgusting conditions, I was sweating like a pig. Since I hadn't had time to shower that morning before leaving to start work, I knew that I probably smelled something like a pig as well.

At eleven thirty Melinda, who was sweating as well, suggested we take a break and go back to her house for lunch. She didn't have to twist my arm to get me to agree. We each took a couple of minutes in the bathroom to wash ourselves a little before we met up in the kitchen. Since she'd worked right along with me all morning, I offered to do anything I could to help get lunch together, which was of course what I was doing when Ben came in from the fields.

I couldn't smell myself, but I had no problem smelling Ben—he smelled like something that had fallen into a pile of manure. And in case you've never smelled manure, on a hot summer day, it's not something you want to be breathing in a confined space. Ben apparently saw me wrinkling my nose, because he asked something rude, which was fine. What I found offensive was how he decided to identify me.

"Oh, did the princess get a whiff of something not to her liking?"

Without stopping to consider the consequences of my actions, one of my feet shot out toward him. The only good thing was that Ben saw my foot coming at him and managed to dodge out of its way.

"Bite me," I told him without missing a beat.

When we all sat down to eat about ten minutes later, Ben smelled a bit fresher. I hadn't stopped sweating yet and most likely wouldn't until probably September at the rate we were going. Before food, I think I inhaled about a gallon of iced tea, including chewing on the ice cubes in my glass.

My afternoon passed much the way the morning had, only I sweated more because we were into the hottest part of the day. Melinda had volunteered her entire morning to help clean, but in the afternoon, she had to work in her roadside farm market. Since my dad had slept in, I left him, I hoped, to do more of the housework while I went to help Melinda at the market. I could not believe how many people stopped in there in the course of an afternoon. We were busy pretty much constantly.

In addition to sweating, the key feature of the afternoon for me was simple: I couldn't tell the difference between some of the vegetables. Case in point, Ben swanned in at one point in the afternoon, of course just when we were slammed with customers, and shouted an order to me to run into the back and bring out more asparagus.

I'm not going to lie—I didn't know an asparagus from an artichoke from an aardvark. I grabbed what I thought was right, which was a green spike thing with lots of little green blebs off the main stalk. I know now that I got it wrong. I knew before I got out there with an armful of them that I had at least a fifty-fifty shot at having the wrong thing in my hands. Ben, the ever so gentle, loving, helpful creature that he was, didn't hesitate for a moment before shouting loud enough for everyone within a mile to hear, "Yo, dumbass, those are Brussels sprouts, not asparagus."

The temptation to take one of the stalks in hand and use it as a baseball bat—with his head as the baseball—was overwhelming. I could hear people laughing (quietly, but still) all over the store. A couple of people scowled at Ben, which felt good. I decided to focus on those folks, giving them my best smile. Melinda scolded Ben, but I think we all knew how effective that was going to be.

At the end of the afternoon when Melinda closed down for the day, I was so grateful, so relieved, so happy that I very nearly fell to my knees in the dirt parking lot to give thanks. I would have, too, except that I was so wet with sweat that I was afraid half of the parking lot would have stuck to me, and that thought was repulsive.

Melinda gave me a ride back to our house and came inside with me for a minute to see how much work my dad had gotten through during our absence. The answer was not much, which didn't surprise me in the least. My dad was good at giving orders but wasn't so good at doing indoor type work. In fact, we couldn't find him anywhere, nor could we find any signs of his having been there. Walking back out the front door we both spotted his car driving up to the door.

"You two have a good afternoon?" he asked as he climbed out of the car.

Melinda answered for us. "Busy. Really, really busy."

"Where've you been?" I asked when he wasn't forthcoming.

"Out buying a new refrigerator."

"Ah, so you decided the old one wasn't gonna cut it?"

"No, Adam, I just felt like throwing $1,500 away."

Okay, so he was in one of his moods. I shut up since I knew there was no winning. Melinda was smart and a quick study. She changed the subject. "I wanted to invite the two of you to join us for dinner in about an hour."

"Oh, Melinda, you don't have to keep feeding us," he protested halfheartedly.

"I know that. It's nice to have the company. Farming is a lonely life."

I didn't know how Melinda did it. She'd worked all day right along beside me, and she still managed to rush back to her house and throw together a fantastic dinner. However she did it, it was a tremendous taste treat in my estimation. Even though I was as exhausted as I think I had ever felt, partly from the heat and partly from the hard physical labor of the day, I couldn't let Melinda clean up. She'd done the work of making dinner and had to be as tired as I was. When she started to get up to pick up the plates and clean up, I stopped her and took over.

Ben, being the prick that he was, chimed in and told his mother, "Yeah, don't you know that cleaning is women's work?" I made a point of shoving the back of his chair one time as I passed, which was a compromise from what I had wanted to do—I had wanted to dump something dirty and disgusting on his head.

On my second pass by the table clearing away the dirty dishes, Ben shoved his empty coffee mug my way and said, "Coffee." I assume that meant he wanted some, but he needed to get it clear that I wasn't there as his personal servant.

"It's in the pot," I muttered.

He shoved the mug in my face again and repeated his order, making sure I could see his pissed-off expression at the same time. After I'd dumped the latest round of dishes in the sink I grabbed the coffee pot and walked back toward the table. When I was about a foot away, Ben still had his cup out waiting. I stopped and stared at him.

Since I knew it would piss him off, I walked around and offered coffee to Melinda first, then my dad, and finally got to Ben. I crowded into his space and stared at him before setting the coffee pot down on the table so he could pour his own.

"You're welcome," I told him as I returned to the sink to wash dishes.

I didn't like what I was hearing coming from the table. "So, Ma, when do I get a chance to get some of that free help you've been talking about?"

"Benjamin, be polite," she chided him. "Tomorrow's Saturday, our busiest day of the week at the roadside stand. On top of that, Becky isn't going to be in tomorrow, so we're already down by one person. If Adam is willing, I'd really like to have his help tomorrow."

"Sure," I told her, "I'd be glad to help you any way I can. Anyone who cooks like this gets whatever she needs," I told her, buttering her up a little in the process while I also tried to piss off Ben.


SO I spent Saturday helping Melinda all day long in the roadside farm stand. And if I thought Friday was busy, that day had nothing on the crowds we saw on Saturday. We opened at 8:00 that morning and spent an hour before that setting up and getting everything staged. And we had people as soon as she unlocked the door. It wasn't until 2:00 in the afternoon that we got a break to so much as pee. And believe me, by then, I was exceptionally in need of going to pee. Not to mention, I was starving. It was odd working around food in its raw form and feeling such hunger. Had we been working with things that were covered with frosting, I'd have been all set, but what could you do with mountains of raw Brussels sprouts when you were hungry? Nothing. That's what.

During a brief pause between customers, I asked Melinda where all the customers were coming from. She told me that she got a lot of people driving between the two biggest cities in the area.

"We also get a lot of locals," she explained.

"But this whole area is farmland. Don't they all grow their own stuff?" I asked.

"Oh, no. Most of the folks who live in the area work somewhere else. There isn't much work around here since the last factory closed. And most of the farming is done by a very small number of people. A few people have a small vegetable garden, but most don't. Most wouldn't know how to grow anything if they tried. So they come to me, and I'm all too happy to sell to them."

Lunch, if you could call it that, was a slab of cheese and an apple along with some bread that we sold in the market. I'm not sure how, but Melinda somehow oversaw another part of the operation that baked a mountain of fresh bread every single day of the week. The bread smelled heavenly during the baking phase of the operation, and since bread was baking all afternoon, it was pretty much a phenomenal smell just when I was the most hungry.

I realized that I needed to come up with a new term for the place. It wasn't a little tiny fruit stand, but was a real, honest-to-goodness store, just a very rustic one built in what I guess was at one time a barn. In addition to the main area where customers browsed and made selections, there were also completely separate rooms that handled the baking and cheese production.

Ben sailed in and out several times during the day, but for once, good fortune was on my side, and he steered completely clear of me. Each time Ben passed through, I got a good look at him. Why the hell did the guy have to look so damned good? He wore jeans that wrapped around his body like a second skin. They fit him like a custom-made glove. They looked to have been worn and washed so many times that they were a faded light blue, which unfortunately only made the body around which they were molded that much more stunning.

Once when he came through, he had little bits of straw in his hair, which only seemed to make him look more innocent and pure. Too bad he opened his mouth, because it sort of killed the illusion of purity.

Ben always wore white T-shirts. It didn't seem to me to be a reasonable color for him to wear given the nature of his work, but it was what he seemed to wear every day. The only problem was the T-shirts were apparently a bit old, because they didn't fit him too well. In other words, they were a little small for him, so they fit him rather tightly. If his jeans were a second skin, I didn't know what his shirts were. I swear, the man's nipples were as sharp as tacks, and they constantly looked like they were going to bore a hole through those tight fitting T-shirts of his. Each time I caught sight of them I had to restrain myself from attaching myself to them, which would have sucked because I hated the man they were attached to. I was so unhappy Ben did that to me. I disliked him and at the same time wanted to hump his leg. I was a bit of a nipple nut. Why was it that such perfect nipples were attached to such a total pig from hell?

Sunday was a repeat of Saturday, only a slight bit slower. We were still sleeping at Melinda's house because one experiment at sleeping on the old beds in the farmhouse next door had shown us that they desperately needed to be replaced with more sanitary mattresses that didn't smell of dead generations and decades.

Since my dad always seemed in a foul mood when he came back from shopping and spending lots of money, I really hated to see him go off on another shopping trip, but only one night attempting to sleep on the old mattress and I was willing to put up with his predictably bad mood. I don't know what the old mattresses were made of, but it felt like something akin to concrete, maybe with some gravel thrown in for good measure. Plus a whole lot of something that stunk.

# Chapter Seven
# Indentured to Ben

THE FIRST day I had to work with Ben was not something I was looking forward to. That day I showed up at the barn, trying to find Ben at what I thought was the proper time. I walked all around, but he was nowhere to be seen. I don't know how he did it, but when I turned around, Ben was standing directly behind me.

"You looking for something, little man?" he asked.

"You," I told him with as much confidence as I could muster.

"Why?" he asked with a hint of a smirk. He knew damned well why I was there. His mother had told him the previous evening at dinner. I'd sat there and listened to the conversation. But if he wanted to play that game, bring it on.

"To see if you needed any help."

Ben had his arms crossed, sending serious "Don't fuck with me" signals.

"I'm a farmer. There's always work to be done."

I stood in front of him, waiting. I was determined to not make this any easier on him than I had to. If he wanted to be a prick, well bring it on—so could I.

"So you've lived your whole life in the city. You ever been on a farm before?" Ben asked.

"Nope. Never."

"Well, here's the way it works. We work sunup to sundown. Be here tomorrow morning at sunup. You were late this morning. I'll work ya', although I doubt you'll make it more than a day." Ben turned and started to walk away, but stopped. "Come on. And get some work clothes. Don't wear none of that frilly shit," he ordered.

"What?" I asked, finally finding my voice and complaining. "What 'frilly shit'? What's wrong with what I'm wearing?" I demanded. I looked down and verified that I was wearing a pair of blue jeans and a T-shirt. Granted it wasn't a white T-shirt like his and my jeans were brand-new and not worn to the thickness of a tissue like his, but they were still jeans and a T-shirt.

"I'm wearing the same thing you are," I complained. "Jeans and a T-shirt."

"If you don't mind getting your good jeans dirty with manure and stuff, then have at it," he told me. "But the shoes have got to go."

I looked down at my sneakers. They were not new, which was why I chose them. I was guessing I'd be doing some nasty things if Ben had anything to say about it, so I didn't want to wear any of my newer shoes.

"What's wrong with my sneakers?" I asked him.

He snickered. "You find out the first time you slip into a pile of manure. Then you'll switch to boots."

It was early, so the heat wasn't too bad yet. That was about the only good thing I could say about that day. The day was not one of my better ones in my sixteen years walking this planet. And why, you might wonder, was my day so awful? Well, let me tell you. It can be summed up in one word: manure.

The Taylor farm didn't keep a lot of animals, but they did have a couple of cows for milk, some chickens, a couple of turkeys, and several horses. I could tell instantly as I followed Ben and watched him that the horses were his favorite. He became a completely different person around them—softer, gentler, cooing to them, brushing them, giving them treats. It was nice to watch.

But then Ben moved the horses out of their stalls and sent them out into a pasture to graze.

"All right," Ben started. "Job number one. Take that shovel, that wheelbarrow, and start cleaning out the horse stalls. Dump it there," he indicated, pointing to a spot a fair distance away. "Take that hose," he pointed to a hose hung perfectly on a peg on the wall, "and hose down the stalls completely." He pointed to a bucket and some chemical of some sort and described how to mix them and then use the mixture to scrub the floors of the stalls. "And then you hose them out again until every hint of the cleaner is gone. There can't be so much as a whiff of it left, or they'll smell it. As I figure it, by then your sneakers will be soaked, and you'll regret having worn them."

I wanted to complain. I wanted to rant and to throw things and swear using every bad word I'd ever heard. But I kept my mouth shut. It was not easy for me to do that. I was a New Yorker, after all. I'd been raised around and by pushy, determined people who knew what they wanted and went after it, not letting anyone or anything get in their way. So keeping my mouth shut was quite an accomplishment.

Following Ben's instructions I shoveled the manure. And allow me to say: *disgusting!*

Who knew horses took such big dumps? I didn't. And they seemed to think nothing of standing in it, walking in it, and generally spreading it around for me to clean up. Since it was my first time, I probably worked slower than Ben would, but I was trying to do a good job and not miss anything. I didn't want to give Ben one bit of ammunition to use against me.

An hour after I started, I called Ben to inspect my work before I put my tools away. The pompous prick actually held his hands behind his back as he walked around and then into each horse stall, checking everything. His face revealed nothing. Finally he said, "If that's the best you can do." He started to walk away, ordering, "Come on."

Fortunately our next chore did not involve manure. Personally I'd had enough of that stuff to last a lifetime. Our next chore involved going out into a field. From what my dad had said while driving up there, I at least knew that we were walking through a field of corn. We stopped in the middle of the field where a loose pile of rocks—small ones and big ones—sat, along with another wheelbarrow, a sledgehammer, and a shovel.

Pointing, Ben ordered, "We need this all removed. It's in the way of machinery."

"What am I supposed to do with it?" I asked.

"Haul all of the rocks out to the edge of the road." He pointed way off into the distance to a road that was farther away than I could believe. "Oh, and you'll need to wear gloves," he told me.

"Where do I find them?"

"You don't have your own?"

"No! Why would I have gloves?"

"Back in the barn."

So I backtracked all the way to the barn, found some gloves and returned to the pile of rocks, then loaded some of the loose ones into the wheelbarrow. When I tried to lift the damned thing, I had to stop and take some of them back out. Who knew rocks weighed so much? Not me, that's for sure. But I do now.

The trek to the road was torture—pure, complete, absolute torture. By the time I got to the roadside and unloaded my load of rocks, my arms were like dead weight. I didn't think I could have lifted them again if I had to. I rested for a few minutes before making the reverse trip. That task was a miserable one. I sweated. I strained. I labored. Breaking apart the bigger rocks took a tremendous amount of work. It took me the remainder of the day to get through the job, but I did it. By the end of the day, I could barely stand, but when Ben came around to check on me, I could tell he was surprised. Ben lived his life on his face, which meant that if he thought it or felt it, I could see it. The man didn't mask what was going on inside his head. So it gave me tremendous pleasure and pride to make him surprised by what I'd accomplished. I could barely move to get back to the barn and then to the house.

At the dinner table that night, I wasn't sure I was even going to be able to lift my arm to handle a knife and fork. Somehow I did it, but don't ask me how, because it's all a bit of a blur. I was more exhausted that night than I think I had ever been before. I was so tired that I did something else I've never done before—I fell asleep at the dinner table. One minute I was sitting there and eating something. The next minute Melinda was shaking me awake and telling me to go upstairs and take a shower. I didn't have to do dishes that night, which was a good thing. Ben had to do them that night, which was a bad thing, because I knew he'd try to take out his frustration with that task on me the first opportunity he got.

# Chapter Eight
# Work, Work, and
# Still More Work

AND THAT was what my life was like that summer. Three days a week I worked in the roadside stand Melinda ran. The place did a phenomenal amount of business, which truly impressed me. It meant that when I worked there, I was kept busy. There was always work to be done, things to be restocked, customers to help with their purchases, and a thousand other tasks.

The days I wasn't helping Melinda, I was stuck with Ben. Day after day he found backbreaking or menial tasks for me to do. I made it a point to never refuse a task he gave me. I might have sworn up a storm inside my mind, but I never gave him the satisfaction of hearing me complain one single bit. He'd expected me to fold after the first day, but I was not about to give him the satisfaction. I was prepared to do just about anything to prove him wrong.

So one day I was moving rocks. Another day I was helping to harvest tomatoes or strawberries or flowers or some other thing they sold at the stand. Another day Ben would have me pulling weeds in fields that seemed to go on forever. Sometimes he had me cleaning out the horse stalls, a task that became especially miserable in the hottest days of the summer. Manure smells bad, but add heat and a closed-in space, and it became truly awful.

So day in and day out, Ben and Melinda kept me busy, working sunup to sundown seven days a week. I don't know what my dad was intending. I hardly ever saw him to talk with him. By the time we moved into our house I was going to work before he got up, and I went to bed almost as soon as I got back each night. So one good thing about this was that I never had to interact much with him. I could live with it that way with no problem.

No matter how hard I worked or how good a job I did, Ben remained his constant miserable self to me. I had no idea why he hated me, but he clearly did. I could walk on water and still most likely not please the man. I did good work, I didn't slack off, but I learned to never expect much from Ben other than criticism and complaints. I tried to treat him as just background noise as much as possible.

The day in mid-July when he said we were going to have to work together the following day just instantly sent me into a bad mood. Usually he saw me in the morning, gave me an assignment, and then disappeared. But my good luck ended when he said, "We need to fix fences tomorrow. Wear your toughest jeans, wear your boots, and wear a long-sleeve flannel shirt to protect your arms. Fencing work is tough and that barbed wire can really hurt."

"In this heat?" He couldn't be serious. It was supposed to be brutally hot tomorrow and he wanted me to put more clothes on? Was he nuts?

"Got work to do rain or shine, hot or cold."

So the next morning I was there on time and ready to go only to have to wait for Ben to show up. I don't know where he was or why he was running late, but he was. When he finally sauntered out of the house, he got us organized and drove us out to a distant part of the farm using an ATV that they kept for getting around the vast expanse of the farm.

I got through the morning. I was cut, bruised, scraped, and damaged in any number of ways, but I got through the morning. We stopped for lunch that Ben had brought with him that morning. It wasn't anything grand, but it gave us nourishment as well as a chance to stop and rest for a few minutes.

The shady spot we had that day was under an old tree. I was leaning back against an old wall that had been built by piling up stones. Someone, sometime through the ages had taken stones from the field and stacked them up to make fences. Maybe I wasn't the first indentured servant to work on the farm.

I was just starting to drift off to sleep when I heard the strangest sound somewhere nearby. I couldn't figure out what it was and was simply too tired to get up and investigate. So you can imagine my surprise when Ben looked my way. I watched his eyes open wide as if startled about something. He held up his hands and said, "Adam, do not move. Listen to me very carefully. Do not move a single muscle. Hold perfectly still until I tell you to move. Please, Adam, this is very important. Listen to me and hold perfectly still."

I was seriously concerned but decided I should do what he directed me to do. I watched him grab a long stick and move toward me, only a little to my right. "Hold perfectly still," he ordered again. I did exactly as he asked. "Don't move. Almost got it. Don't move. Don't turn. Don't even breathe." Who was he kidding? I had to breathe. He started poking gently with the stick and I heard the sound again, only a little more distant—no longer right beside my head.

"Okay, Adam, get up now! Fast."

I jumped and moved over to stand behind him. "What the fuck was going on?" I asked.

He pointed to a big snake on the top of the stone wall. "Rattler," he said, as if that meant anything to me.

"Huh?"

"Rattlesnake. Their bite can kill."

I felt the blood drain from my face, and I got light-headed as I watched the monster slither away. It must have been right near my head, probably inches from where I'd been sitting. I grabbed Ben to keep myself upright. I must have looked faint because Ben was for once a decent human being.

"It's okay. It's over. You're okay. No harm done."

I put my head down and tried to breathe, to get some oxygen to my brain. Eventually my light-headedness passed. I guess I still looked a bit panicked, because Ben kept telling me that I was safe.

"I didn't know those things lived this far north."

"Not many left anymore. I haven't seen one in quite a while, but I guess we've got a couple around here again."

"Fuck, fuck, fuck," I swore softly. "I want to go home so bad. I hate it here."

I'd been careful to never reveal anything of a personal nature to Ben, and there I'd just gone and spilled a whole lot of personal stuff, or at least given him clues to a lot. He knew I was there against my will if he listened to what I'd said.

We went back to our fence work, me with my eyes constantly on the lookout for more of the monsters like the one that had nearly killed me. Ben saw and laughed, but kept me busy with fence work. He'd hammer and I'd unroll the wire. Both jobs were miserable. The fencing I was hauling was heavy. My clothes were hot. I was hot. We were both in the direct sun at the hottest time of the day. I was sweating like a pig, assuming pigs could sweat. That was bad enough, but then I noticed that I stopped sweating. I felt weird. It got hard to figure out how to work the fence, the roll of wire I'd been working with all day. I didn't understand what was going on. And then there was nothing.

And then I was on the ground, flat on my back with Ben standing over me slapping my face. Wait a minute. What? Where... where was I? Why did I feel so freaking funny? Why was Ben slapping my face? Everything was fuzzy and nothing was clear.

One minute I was on the hard ground, and then—don't ask me how—I was floating. No, I was flying. Wow. I was flying through the air. Oh, the feel of the air flowing over and around me was fantastic. My head lolled back. I hope I didn't need to do anything to stay aloft because I didn't have the focus to do much of anything.

Then I saw Ben again. How did he get there? Was he flying too? Ben looked... stressed, I guess. He looked... maybe worried. No. It was more than that. Ben was close to panic. Yes. I'm sure of it.

Oh, wait, I wasn't flying. Ben had me. Ben was carrying me. Okay. That made more sense. Or did it? Ben hated me. Why would Ben carry me anywhere?

We moved from the blazing hot sunlight into a copse of trees that provided shade to a small pocket of land in the field. The lack of sun felt so fucking good. I heard something. Oh no, not another... another what? I don't know. It was water. I heard running water. Were we back at the house? How did Ben do that?

Not only did I hear the water bubbling somewhere as it moved, but then I suddenly felt it. I was sinking into some of the most exquisite cold water anyone on the planet had ever gone into—ever. I figured out that Ben was in that water with me. He was holding me. I was sure of it now. He still had that look of panic on his face. He was using his big hands to scoop up some of the water and pour it over my head and face. More of the delicious water was poured over my torso. I had that damned long-sleeved shirt on, which was absorbing water like mad. My body was starting to weigh more and it was hard for me to move my limbs.

I closed my eyes and rested in Ben's arms. He continued to pour water over me. I was starting to feel better. What the fuck had happened?

"Ben?" I asked, speaking my first words.

"I've got you, Adam. I've got you. Don't worry. How are you feeling?"

"Weird. Dizzy. What... what happened?"

"Heat stroke. You overheated. I'm trying to cool you off."

"Where are we?" I asked him, turning my head to look around at least a little bit.

"We're in my own secret swimming hole."

There was nothing about that sentence that was upsetting. So why was I crying? I didn't understand, but I was leaning my head against Ben's broad chest and I was crying.

"What's wrong?" Ben quietly asked.

I shook my head the best I could, but eventually croaked out one word, "Everything."

"What?" Ben asked, trying to be soft spoken. I guess he was afraid of something, although I didn't know what.

"My entire life is such a fucked-up mess."

"It's okay. Don't worry about it. Let's get you cooled off and feeling better. One thing at a time. Okay?"

"Okay."

I tried to stand a bit, aided by Ben. I was shaky, but I was able to at least remain upright.

"We need to get out of these wet clothes," Ben commented as casually as he would ask me to pass the potatoes at dinner.

Before my very eyes, Ben was slipping out of his shirt. I had essentially seen the man's upper body through one of those white T-shirts that always seemed to be just about one size too small for him. I didn't know if he had just bought the wrong size or he had grown since they were originally purchased.

It was Ben's typical pattern to shed the shirt in the afternoon when we worked outside. So I had seen his trim, tight torso countless glorious times. There probably wasn't an inch of his visible torso that I had not examined discreetly and studied, some repeatedly. I can honestly say, after hours of careful study and analysis, it was a toss-up for me which feature I liked best about Ben's body. His abs looked like they had been carved out of granite. I'd heard about eight-pack abs and had seen some pictures of them, but I'd never seen any in the flesh, so to speak. Ben clearly had an eight pack, and let me tell you, they were a work of art. Ben's abs were magical to me. I wanted to just reach out and caress them every time I saw them. I'd jerked off over the memory of those abs some nights.

Of course there were also those nipples of his. I swear that at times it seemed like those nipples never softened but were perpetually on high alert, trying to poke holes through his T-shirt. And when he took his shirt off, I had all I could do not to run up to him and lock my lips on his perky nipples, worrying them with my tongue until he cried out for mercy. I'd jerked off over those nipples as well.

It didn't matter how hard I tried, and I did try, I couldn't help but stare as he started to push his wet jeans down off his hips. With every inch of fresh flesh that came into view, I was that much more concerned that I was going to lose it—totally. I was convinced I was about to simply implode from pent up sexual energy and frustration.

Since everything he wore was wet, when he pushed his jeans down off his hips, his underwear went with them. It took him more work than usual to get his jeans off because they were so wet. He was positioned partially away from me so what I primarily saw was his butt. And oh, let me tell you, if I had liked what was above the beltline, what was below was ten times better. I wasn't sure how it was humanly possible, but Ben's body just kept getting better and better.

First there was an ass that could only be described as perfection. I swear that Michelangelo didn't leave us with anything as good as Ben's ass. I watched Ben struggle with getting his boots unlaced and off so he could remove his jeans the rest of the way. It took some work, and I thought he was going to lose his balance once, but he managed to get the offending footwear off.

Leaning up against a tree, Ben finally got both of his legs free from the offending jeans. I watched with my mouth hanging partially open as the man wrung out his wet jeans and took them about twenty feet away to lay them in a place that was in the full sun.

He was saying something, but I didn't have a clue what it was. The next thing I knew, Ben was standing in front of me. "Hey, you okay?" he asked.

"Um, yeah. I guess."

"You look a little dazed."

I shook my head. "Still a bit out of it, I guess," I told him. Accepting that answer, Ben walked around, seeming to examine the area for a good place to park himself.

"Why are you being so human to me? You hate me."

"I don't hate you," Ben told me softly. "Quite the opposite. Come on. Get those wet clothes off and come sit with me," he ordered.

"I can't," I told him.

"Come on," Ben ordered. "Strip."

"I can't," I tried once again to explain, but it didn't work any better that time than it had the time before.

"Yes, you can. You need to get out of those wet clothes or you're going to be miserable. You're going to be chafed, and your skin is going to be beat to shit. Trust me, I know, so get 'em off," Ben ordered.

With great hesitation, I started to shed my clothes, which now weighed a ton because they had absorbed so much water from my little dip in the creek. It wasn't easy, but I got the pants off, struggling to keep my underwear firmly in place. That last thing I needed was for farmer boy to see me pop a woodie from checking out his ass. He'd take one look at me and I'd be checking into an early grave—and he'd be putting me there.

Emulating Ben's move, I tried to wring the water out of my jeans and then took them over to lie in the sun along with my boots and shirt. My underwear remained firmly in place. I would never admit it, but wearing wet underwear felt absolutely miserable. Had I been alone I would have shed the underwear in a heartbeat. I'd always liked being naked, and there was some special thrill that went along with being naked outside. Between Ben's glorious body and the thrill of being naked outdoors, I had no doubt that my seventeen-year-old penis would instantly spring to life and ask to come out and play too.

Ben had parked himself beneath a large tree so he was in dappled sunlight, but mostly shaded. Hesitantly I walked over and sat down near him. He had his legs extended, one leg crossed over the other, leaning back and supporting his torso on his two arms, which were extended out behind him so his torso was at a forty-five degree angle. As if that wasn't bad enough, he had his head thrown back and his eyes closed. Good Lord! Didn't the man know that he was like a little piece of heaven sent down to earth?

My eyes were drawn to his body like a magnet to metal. I should have expected it, but Ben's legs and penis were every bit as lovely as his upper body had been. I really shouldn't have been surprised. I had so much more Ben to study now. I tried to look at all of him before he opened his eyes and caught me. There was just so much wonder to take in.

I was so absorbed in studying Ben's classic physique that I jumped in surprise when he spoke.

"I haven't been in the stream yet this summer," Ben explained out of the blue, uttering perhaps the most words he had to me in one sentence that didn't involve some order or command.

"You swim here often—other years?" I asked.

"Used to all the time each summer. Too much work now with my dad gone."

"You want to borrow mine?" I asked. "You can keep him if you want."

"Why's he so pissed off at you?" Ben asked, which was the first interest Ben had ever seemed to take in me beyond being an indentured servant to him and his farm.

"What makes you think he's pissed off at me?" I asked.

"Doesn't take a genius to see that you two have some... what do they call them? Issues?"

How the hell should I answer that one? Turns out I didn't have to because Ben figured it out for me.

"Is it because you like guys?"

I shot to my feet. *Oh fuck, oh fuck, oh fuck.* How the hell had he figured that out? I knew it. I knew I shouldn't have stared at him so much. Damn. He must have seen me. Oh, I was so fucking screwed.

With my heart pounding at double-time, I managed to stammer, "What? What are you talking about?"

Ben wasn't flustered in the least. With the same calm he'd had before he'd asked his question, he remained unmoved. He sat on the ground talking as casually as if he was discussing what was on television that evening.

He raised his head and stared at me. "I said, is it because you like guys?"

"I... I heard you the first time," I told him angrily. "What makes you say something like that?"

"Easy." The man was so freaking calm it was driving me nuts.

"Yeah? How?"

"All I had to do was watch you."

I was stunned. How in the world had this backwoods farmer figured out my deepest, darkest secret?

"You trying to figure out how some hick from the sticks figured you out so easily?"

I stared. The man was... I don't know. He wasn't the man I thought I'd been working with all this time. The man in front of me, asking these questions was... well, perceptive, thoughtful, insightful.

The man I'd been taking orders from for weeks was a tyrant—a seemingly dim-witted tyrant.

Since there was apparently no chance of getting anything past this mystery man, I decided to just answer him directly. "Yes."

Rather than continue our conversation, Ben sat on the ground, as casual and as relaxed as could be—and naked, don't forget the naked part—and just stared at me. His face was relaxed. I can't say that he was smiling, but he certainly wasn't frowning or sneering at me like he had when we first met.

I had naturally dropped my gaze to the ground rather than risk looking at Ben. When I did dare to glance up quickly I found his eyes locked on mine. Oddly enough, though, his face didn't reveal the anger I had anticipated.

"What?" I demanded, still standing.

"I didn't say anything," he answered, still staring at me and looking exasperatingly unruffled.

I stared at him for a moment, trying to figure out what his game was.

"What? No smart comment?" I demanded.

"No. Why should I?"

"You... you don't? Why not? Don't you have some problem with gay people?"

"No. Should I?"

I didn't know what Ben's game was, but I was feeling completely off-base and out of my element. I jumped when a moment later Ben leaped to his feet and patted my arm. "Come on. Get that wet underwear off. It hurts me just to look at you still wearing them. Let's cool off in the stream."

I stared at him. Whatever game he was playing, he was good. And until I figured it out, I didn't move.

"Hey," he said, grabbing my attention once again, more gently than I would have anticipated. "Come on. It's hotter than blue blazes out here. You remember how good that water felt?"

I nodded but kept my mouth shut.

"So get 'em off and get in here with me."

I wanted to argue, but I couldn't. Since his back was turned as he stepped toward the water, I quickly shoved my underwear off and moved to the stream. When I started for one spot, he stopped me. "No. Come over here."

"Why?" I asked suspiciously.

"Trust me" was all he said.

I didn't, but I also didn't see an alternative, so I went to where he stood. He got into the water, but turned back and offered one of his hands to me. With no other option, I took his hand, and he guided me to something I had not seen before. Whether arranged by man or nature, there were two rock "seats" submerged under the water line of the small creek.

He took one of the spots, and I ducked down and took the other, which unfortunately was fairly close to Ben. My leg touched his accidentally, and I quickly tried to jerk it away. The only problem was that there just wasn't enough room to make such a move.

"Is this your doing?" I asked him.

"What? The seats? Yeah. Did it years ago."

"So this is a favorite spot of yours?"

"Yep. Far enough away from the house and the barn that no one ever comes out here unless they're working the fields near here. When I was growing up, I tried to get out here all the time when summer hit. I've always found it to be a great way to cool off."

And then he shocked me even more.

"I learned how to jerk off sitting right here."

What, exactly, does one say to someone when they confess a thing like that to you? Right. I didn't have a fucking clue, so I just stared at him.

"You look just like a deer caught in the headlights of a pickup truck on a back road at night."

"That good, huh?"

He chuckled at me. The goddamned son of a bitch actually chuckled at me, or more accurately, he chuckled at my discomfort.

"I'm so glad I could entertain you," I told him, struggling to get up and get out of the water. I didn't make it very far, though, before I felt his strong hands on my shoulders gently pulling me back down into the water.

"Stay, please," he asked. Try as I might, I could not find a single threatening thing in his words or in the tone of voice he used when he spoke. Casting one more quick, suspicious glance his way, I settled back into the spot where I had been sitting.

"Now, wasn't I right?" he asked me.

"About what? About you learning to jerk off here? I wouldn't know. I've never seen you jerk off before, and certainly not when you were learning how to do it, unless you were a late bloomer." I don't know what it was that made me so ballsy, but I heard myself saying those words before my brain could filter them out. Maybe I was just trying to find some footing so I could get the upper hand again, assuming I'd ever had it in the first place. And then, wouldn't you know it? He took the upper hand in ways I didn't see coming.

# Chapter Nine
# "I'd Really Like to Kiss You"

"I'D REALLY like to kiss you," Ben said to me. I felt my eyes bug out so much that it was a miracle they didn't just pop right out of my head. Ben chuckled at me once again but didn't wait for an answer. Instead, he just leaned in toward me and—more gently than I would ever have anticipated—touched his lips to mine. Ben's kiss was hesitant, tentative. It was also the first move I'd seen from the man that hadn't been cocky and know-it-all assured.

His lips weren't the only part of his body that touched me, though. While his lips gently touched mine, I felt his hand on my leg. Ben's hands were large. I'd noticed that the first time I met him. As it turned out, all of Ben was large, from his big hands to his height to his big feet... oh, and also his big dick. You see, when Ben touched my leg, my hand sort of instinctively went to his leg. Only I seemed to overshoot a little in my exuberance and instead of grabbing his leg I suddenly found myself with a handful of rapidly expanding Ben-cock. When it finally stopped getting larger Ben's penis made one hell of an impressive presence.

"Wow," I said breathlessly.

"Wow?" he asked.

"Yeah, wow."

"What wow? The kiss? My dick? The water?"

"Yes," I answered him. Before he could ask anything more, I quickly moved so I was on top of him with one knee on each side of his hips. I leaned in and immediately locked my lips to his. Only I didn't stop there. The calm Ben had showed somehow leaped across the short distance from him to me. Now he looked edgy, and I was calm.

With one hand on each side of his head, my fingers threaded their way into Ben's silky soft hair. He kept his hair cut short, so there wasn't much for me to work with, but I did my damnedest to get a grip on something and hold his face to mine so we could kiss without interruption.

My tongue probed his mouth, demanding entrance like a soldier pummeling the gates of an enemy's fortress. Ben didn't fight me. If anything, he fell limply backward and let me do whatever I wanted. And what I wanted was to kiss the stuffing out of him.

But then I remembered. Oh, fuck! This was how the nightmare I was living had started. I couldn't do that again. Oh, fuck! I pulled back and gasped for air. Apparently I looked a little wild, because Ben had a startled look and asked me, "What did I do? What's wrong? I won't do it again. I promise."

I jumped back away from him and in the process somehow my foot slipped on something slick in the bottom of the creek. I started to cry out just when my body hit the water, which meant that I inhaled what felt like a lungful of water. But that wasn't the worst of it. No, I had to go and make it worse by somehow getting my foot wedged between two rocks or something rock-like, which meant that when I tried to cough up the water all I did was to take on more. I couldn't breathe and I desperately needed to breathe. I had to get air and since I couldn't, I started to panic. Crap, I was going to die. My dad finding me kissing Mark last time wasn't bad enough? This time my punishment was death? This just sucked.

Fear and not being able to breathe had me in such a panic that I was thrashing around even more, in the process consuming more of my very limited oxygen supply. But then everything started to get kind of foggy. I wasn't as much in a panic anymore as I mellowed out. The last thing I remembered was a feeling of peacefulness as the water blanketed me and seemed to rock me to sleep.

The next thing I knew, I was gasping for air and coughing hard enough to hack up a lung. I rolled onto my side and kept coughing, spitting up water. I rolled again and raised myself, heaving.

When I had expelled all of the water I could, along with just about everything else in my stomach, I had a whole new range of pain.

Now, in addition to the burning in my lungs, all the muscles in my sides and my abdomen hurt. Moving was painful. Breathing was painful. Hell, blinking my eyes was painful.

I collapsed onto the ground and closed my eyes as I focused on one thing and one thing only: breathing. I just wanted to lie there and go to sleep, or at least not move so maybe I wouldn't hurt so much. But I couldn't do that because Ben was in the middle of his own personal panic attack. I tuned back in to the sound of his voice in time to hear him pleading, "Please, please, please don't die. Oh, God. I'm so sorry. I'm so very sorry. Please, please don't die. No. Please. Please stay with me."

I turned my head enough to be able to look at him and mutter, "Shut up and let me suffer in silence."

"Are you okay?" Ben asked, looking terrified.

"What do you think?" I asked. "No, I'm not all right. I—" Coughing interrupted my explanation. "Fuck!" I complained. "That hurts so bad." I think I shed a few tears. Put the whole picture together and I'm sure I looked like a complete fucking mess, certainly anything but attractive and desirable.

I felt one of Ben's large hands on my head, gently stroking my hair. His other hand was resting on my back between my shoulder blades.

"Are you comfortable?" he asked me.

I groaned, which led to a coughing spell, which in turn led to another groan.

Ben shifted himself so he could pull my head against his chest. He had me propped between his legs, holding my body at a forty-five degree angle so I could breathe without putting me in too much pain. If it hadn't been for the spikes of pain with each breath, I'd actually have liked being held in Ben's strong arms. Too bad I couldn't enjoy the experience.

We stayed like that for a long time. I think I slept a bit, but through it all, Ben remained perfectly still, holding me, stroking my hair, giving me a pillow to rest against. I have no idea how much time passed before I heard Ben trying to rouse me. "Adam. Come on, Adam, I need you to wake up now. Adam? Can you hear me? Time to wake up."

"Go 'way," I muttered.

"Sorry, but it's time to get up. We need to head back to the house. I don't want to be out here after dark trying to find our way back without any lights."

That last statement was enough to wake me up the rest of the way. Ben helped to push me more upright. Somehow he got to his feet and then helped me to get to mine. "Where...?" I started to ask, not even sure what I was trying to ask.

"Our clothes are over there," Ben told me, pointing to where we'd put our clothes to dry in the sun.

I mumbled something unintelligible. Ben helped me to walk toward our clothes, then took his hands off me only long enough to bend over and pick up my pants. My underwear was still a bit damp but my jeans were mostly dry, which surprised me—I would have anticipated just the opposite. I didn't care, though, so I pulled on my jeans and shoved my underwear in my pocket. Both pairs of boots were somewhat dry but not entirely, which felt absolutely awful. Our compromise was that we didn't lace our boots back up but left them loose.

It took every ounce of energy I had, but I followed Ben as he led us back to where he'd parked the ATV we'd driven out to the field that morning. By the time we got back to the vehicle, I was winded and whipped. Ben got me seated and then drove us back to his house as quickly as possible. I don't know if it was the way Ben drove, some gesture he made, or the way I looked, but before we'd even stopped, Ben's mother was running toward us.

"What happened?" she asked.

I was aware enough to see that Ben was shaking. I felt so bad for the poor guy.

"He... he...," Ben tried.

"Ben saved my life," I told her.

"What happened?"

I waited for Ben to pick up the story, but when he didn't I tried. "I passed out. The heat got to me. I thought I was going to die. Ben carried me to a stream and put me in the water to try to cool me off. I got scared and pulled away. I slipped on something and fell into the water. My foot got caught and I couldn't pull loose. I took in a lot of water. I don't really know how I made it out of there, so I guess Ben got me out. Ben saved me."

"You look like crap," she told me, cutting through the pleasantries and right to the heart of the matter.

"Matches how I feel." I couldn't disagree with her.

"Get inside the house," she ordered, "and I'll call your father to come pick you up."

"He's not there," I told her, suddenly remembering his plans for the day. "He left really early this morning and drove into New York for the day. He won't be back until late tonight," I told her. It just sucked that all of this had happened on a day when I actually would have had time to do something with Ben.

Ben didn't contradict his mother but directed me toward the house.

"I can walk," I told him as he tried to herd me.

"I know," he said softly.

Their house wasn't any more air-conditioned than ours was, but they didn't keep their house locked up like my dad did ours. He was a man of the city even though we were living in the country now, so he behaved like a city dweller, which meant you locked your house, closed your windows, and were always on guard against anything unexpected.

Ben's mom, though, had windows open throughout the house, both upstairs and downstairs, so while it was hotter than hell outside, inside there was a nice breeze and the air wasn't completely oppressive. Melinda was tight on Ben's heels. When Ben tried to guide me toward the sofa, Melinda contradicted his decision.

"No, take him upstairs and get him into bed." Then she immediately contradicted herself. "Hells bells, I haven't made up the bed in the spare bedroom. Shoot. Damn."

"The sheets on my bed are clean—I'll just put him there."

"Okay. Do it."

I could almost feel the spirit of my father chafing and screaming out at the thought of me crawling into another man's bed, especially after kissing and making out with said man just a few hours earlier. If only the making out hadn't ended so dismally that said man probably would never want to do anything with me ever again for the remainder of all time.

Upstairs, Ben helped me to slip out of my still dampish clothes. He held the sheets up for me to slide into his bed. I couldn't believe it when I caught a glimpse of him checking out my body. Why in the world he would still want to even look at me was a mystery. If I hadn't been quite so embarrassed by what I'd done earlier and what Ben must think of me, I would have loved to talk with him about it, but that wasn't going to happen. You see, I was so worn down, beat down, used up by everything that had happened today, and Ben's bed was so comfortable, I felt myself drifting off to sleep in almost no time at all.

The sun had been setting when I lay down. When I woke up some time later, the house was dark and quiet. That was all well and good, but I desperately needed to pee. My bladder was beyond desperate in telling me that it needed to happen—*now*! I tried to remember the layout of Ben's bedroom and whether he had his own bathroom. I couldn't remember, so I swung my legs over the side of his bed and felt around to see if there might be a light of some sort beside his bed. That problem resolved, I made my way across the room to open his door into the hallway to go to the bathroom I'd used when I'd stayed there before.

My bladder and I were finally on speaking terms again a couple of minutes later, which was good because when I opened the bathroom door to make my way back to the bedroom, I ran straight into someone. It wouldn't have been very manly, but I very nearly shrieked in surprise. But when I heard Ben's voice I immediately calmed down.

"Sorry," he whispered to me.

"For what?" I asked, also keeping my voice low. "Why are we whispering?"

"My mom's gone to bed."

"Oh, sorry."

"Come on," he ordered, guiding me back into his room. I'd needed to go so badly that I had overlooked one important thing: I was naked. It was such a good thing that I hadn't run into Ben's mom in the hallway. Even though the moment had passed, I still blushed at the mere thought of how awful that would have been.

"You hungry?" Ben asked when he heard my stomach growl.

"Yeah, I guess I am."

I watched Ben rummaging around in his dresser for something for me to wear. A moment later he tossed a pair of shorts my way. On him they would have been fairly tight, but on me they were less so. They were baggy, but at least they weren't falling off me.

Taking me by the hand, Ben led me down the dark hallway to the stairs and then down the stairs to the living room. It was still hot, but it felt much less stifling than it had earlier in the day. There were lights on in the living room, which surprised me. It was only then that I noticed something I should have noticed earlier—Ben was dressed in a pair of loose cut-off shorts—shorts that had become threadbare over the years as first long pants and then as shorts.

I had never seen Ben in shorts before—they looked good on him. When I say Ben was wearing shorts, I should clarify and explain that Ben was wearing shorts and nothing else. Ben was shirtless. It was a very good thing that his mother had gone to bed because between his hand holding mine and his lack of clothing, Ben was doing a real number on my libido. In other words, mentally I had the boner to end all boners. Physically I wasn't that far behind.

"Is your mother a sound sleeper?" I asked Ben.

"Yeah, why?"

"I wouldn't want her to walk in right about now and see what you're doing to me."

"What do you mean?"

I gestured at my crotch, and it only took him one glance to understand. Even though his shorts were loose on me, they were still obviously tented out from my physical reaction to his proximity.

Ben led me into the kitchen and seated me at the table, then produced something to eat—I tasted it, but I couldn't tell you what it was. I was too taken with Ben's beautiful body to be able to tell anything about something so trivial as food. Watching Ben's muscular body move around the kitchen with the style and grace of a ballerina was a true joy. Take him out of his work clothes and his work boots, clean him up, and you had an entirely different person. While farmer Ben was hot, this Ben was handsome and hunky and hot. This Ben wasn't as rough as farmer Ben. This Ben moved with a grace that belied his six-foot-tall frame. And this Ben didn't seem to be perpetually angry or short-tempered with me, and that alone was something of note.

As I sat there that evening, I honestly wondered if I had imagined the whole kiss thing. It all felt like a dream, like a fairy tale. Over the last six weeks, I had come to believe that good was not for me, but was something reserved for other people. After working seven days a week doing back-breaking work, having no time to relax or do anything, having no time to be with friends, I had quite honestly come to doubt that anything good could or would happen to me again. So I sat there looking at Ben, wondering if I had dreamed the whole thing.

"Was it a dream?" I said aloud.

"Was what a dream?" Ben asked, turning toward me.

"You."

Ben's look alone told me the answer to that question. He smiled at me and sort of cocked his head off to one side a little bit, which only made him more endearingly cute. How was it that I had never seen this Ben before? I liked this Ben. Hell, I had a hard-on for this Ben and despite feeling like warmed-over day-old dog crap, I wanted to throw this Ben to the floor, climb on top of him, and do wild and crazy things to him.

Whatever Ben had been doing was abandoned, and he immediately moved to stand in front of me, separated by only the width of the table.

"The kiss?" Ben whispered to me.

I nodded.

"No, it wasn't a dream. It was real, but I can assure you I'll be dreaming about it for years to come."

"You've… you've kissed guys before, right?" I asked, convinced that he had.

Ben shook his head, his expression transforming to one of dejection in the span of a few seconds. "No," he whispered. "I've kissed a couple of girls—"

"Not the same thing," I interrupted him.

"That's the damned truth," he said, his happy face back in place.

We were both quiet for a moment, and then Ben asked me something that I guess had been on his mind—it had been on mine. "What happened out there? Did I do something wrong? Wasn't I good at it? I'm sorry if—"

"Ben!" I told him, softly but firmly. "You didn't do anything wrong. The problem was me."

"What? You didn't want to kiss me?"

"No, I wanted to kiss you and lick every inch of your body and make you cum without even touching yourself."

"Then what? I don't get it. You pulled back so hard… and you know what happened after that."

Now it was my turn to look down and feel dejected. With a deep sigh, I launched into my explanation, in a roundabout way.

"You know we'd never lived here before my dad brought me up here about six weeks ago."

"Right."

"Well, what you don't know is why he brought me up here." Ben's gaze at me was one of wide-eyed youthful innocence that I found to be absolutely adorable on his face but also a bit out of place. All I'd ever seen on Ben's face before that day was anger and hostility, so seeing anything remotely resembling something positive was all new.

"You see, my dad was supposed to be out of the house one evening—everybody was supposed to be out of the house that night. My best friend, Mark, and I were going to use the time to… um, try some new things." I blushed. Shit. I could feel my cheeks getting red, which only embarrassed me that much further.

"So Mark and I were in my room on my bed." I couldn't believe how wide Ben's eyes became. He was clearly hanging on my every word. "All we were doing was kissing." Without realizing I was doing it, I dropped my voice when I said the word "kissing."

"Were you... did you have your clothes on?" Ben asked me.

"Yes. We had everything on still. I had Mark's pants unbuckled and my hands on his ass, but otherwise we were completely dressed."

"What happened?" he asked.

"My bedroom door flew open, the light came on, and my dad stood there, as shocked to see us as we were to see him. Mark freaked. He absolutely freaked. He... it was awful. He was in an absolute panic. He shoved me and took off running like his feet were on fire.

"Mark wouldn't speak to me again after that. He was so terrified that my dad was going to tell his dad what he'd seen Mark doing with me. When I tried to talk to him, he punched me. He actually punched me in the face right in front of his house. Then he took up with some clueless girl that he actually thought was going to provide him some cover. I lost my best friend.

"So my dad thought the city was corrupting me and that by getting me out of there and out here in the country, he would remove all temptation from me. And I guess he thought I'd just come out here, breathe that country air, work like a big farm animal, and never be tempted by thoughts of a naked man ever again. I'm not about to tell him again, but that's not the way it works."

Ben laughed along with me on that one. "Well," he said, "his plan hasn't worked out quite as well as he'd hoped."

"Let's not tell him that," I said with a sly smile.

"Deal," Ben agreed. "So why did you pull back so suddenly in the swimming hole?"

"I was really shocked and was so fired up. I was getting into it— and I had this sudden image of my dad and that door swinging open and my whole life falling apart. I panicked. I pulled back, afraid he was going to pop up and pull us apart and take me away somewhere else. And you know what happened then."

Ben nodded, seeming to understand my story without further explanation.

Now it was my turn to ask him a question or two.

"Does... does your mom know?"

"About me?"

I nodded.

"No. I don't think so. She's never said anything."

"Have you... um, dated a lot?"

"Like, girls?" he asked, curling his lip slightly.

I nodded.

"I did some, just because if I didn't, everybody would talk. But when my dad died, I had a perfect excuse—I had to work twice as hard here on the farm."

I was going to say something profound and insightful but found myself yawning instead. Ben chuckled and told me, "Come on. Let's get you back to bed. You've had one hell of a day."

"Damn, but that's the truth."

Ben led me back up the stairs and to his bedroom. He got me settled into bed again but then started to leave.

"Ben, please, stay." I hoped it wasn't coming across quite as needy as it sounded, but I was desperate to feel his body next to mine.

"I shouldn't. What if my mom caught us or heard us? And you need to sleep."

"Please." I was not above begging if it would get me what I wanted—Ben in bed with me.

After going through some intense internal debate, Ben nodded, but dashed out of the room. He was back less than sixty seconds later and closed the bedroom door. I heard what sounded like a lock, which was absolute music to my ears.

"Had to turn off the lights downstairs," Ben explained as he shed his cut-offs. One shove and he was completely naked. And what a vision he was as he walked toward the bed. I swear that time seemed to slow down as I watched him, a vision of beauty and loveliness all rolled up into one package—one incredibly masculine package.

Ben's bed was a big one. I don't know what it was, but it was bigger than a double bed. So even though Ben was a big guy, at least compared to me, we had no problem both fitting into the bed, especially with some of the things we had in mind for that night.

By the time Ben reached the other side of the bed and started to slip under the covers to join me, his penis was fully erect. While he rearranged the covers, I did the natural thing and reached out to grab his rigid erection, using it to pull him forward and closer to me.

Our lips naturally sought out their counterparts, and we resumed where we'd stopped earlier in the day—before I'd almost died from drowning. Ben's hands on my body felt like the touch of an angel—soft and gentle yet firm and powerful, capable of moving mountains and at the same time capable of the most tender of caresses.

We kissed with an unbridled intensity. I heard Ben softly moan. And I know I moaned. How could any man feel what I was feeling and keep silent? I didn't think it was possible. Ben's hands on my body, his tongue in my mouth, repeated worried glances from his beautiful eyes. All of it combined to make me one of the happiest men on the planet at that moment in time.

Life can be cruel sometimes. That night was a prime example. I was horny beyond belief, and I was in bed naked with a hunk. But I'd nearly inhaled a couple quarts of water that day and felt like I'd run a marathon as well. In other words, I wanted to hump Ben into a coma, but I was also falling asleep. I wanted to do a whole host of unspeakable things with him right then and there. But without talking about it, we seemed to reach a shared conclusion that there would be time to do all of those things, just not that night.

So after some intense making out, with kisses I swore I'd dream about for days and days, we both curled up tightly together and closed our eyes. And that was the last thing I remember from that day.

# Chapter Ten
# The Oddity of Life

LIFE CAN be funny at times—funny weird, not funny ha-ha. What was odd for me was when I woke up in the morning, the first thing I noticed was a smell—Ben's smell in particular. And yes, Ben had a smell. Now, don't get me wrong. His smell wasn't bad—quite the opposite. Ben had a gloriously masculine scent. It's hard to describe. He was a combination of soap, sweat, sex, and some kind of hair shampoo that I really liked. So, yes, Ben had a distinct smell. I could tell who was with me before I'd even opened my eyes.

Never in a million years would I have ever pictured me in bed with Ben, and especially not with Ben as we were arranged when I woke up. I was lying on my back, slightly propped up against the head of the bed with Ben curled up safely in the crook of my left arm. My left arm was wrapped protectively around him, my left hand gently coasting over his side as if to confirm that what I was sensing was really true.

Ben was taller than me, outweighed me, and had more muscles than me, and he was the one curled up like a sweet young innocent with his head on my chest. It was a beautiful way to wake up and an image I'll keep in my mind forever.

I needed to be sure to not tell him this, but big, tough, scary Ben looked like a vulnerable adolescent—an innocent adolescent—while he slept. The position in which one sleeps can be very telling. That morning, Ben was curled up against me in the cutest semifetal position, with one of his arms across my torso.

My definition of a good day would be one in which I got to lounge naked in bed with a man as hot as Ben. Even though I wasn't going to get to do exactly that, I was still hoping to have a good day, maybe even a great day. Everything had changed in an unbelievably short span of time. But for once, the change was all for the better.

As soon as I started to stir, my movements started to wake Ben. If it turned out he was one of those people who loved mornings—early mornings in particular—I was going to have to reconsider everything good I'd just been thinking about him because in my book early mornings were an evil to be endured.

Although waking up in bed next to a naked Ben might change mornings into an entirely wonderful experience. The sight of him looking so innocent and vulnerable, the smell of his masculinity, and the touch of his body beneath my fingers—the combination was enough to make any guy willing to wake up at any hour of the morning.

After rousing a bit, Ben seemed to settle back down, so I had to gently try to wake him.

"Ben?" I said as I caressed his side a bit more aggressively.

He'd heard me because he groaned or mumbled something. I couldn't tell what he was trying to say, but I didn't care because he was in my arms and for that moment all was well with the world. But I needed to get him to wake up.

"Ben. Time to get up. We need to get up. Does your mom know you were going to sleep here with me last night?" That had him awake. Stretching, which helped him to wake up, flexing his gorgeous body in ways that had other parts of me waking up as well. Damn, but the guy was hot!

"I'm up," he told me, and he was—at least the part of him that was rubbing up against my left leg was definitely up. Too bad we couldn't deal with that, but there was no time. If Ben's mother was going to freak at the idea of finding her son in bed with the neighbor farm help, things were not going to end well for me—for us, probably.

Ben went from sleep to awake remarkably quickly. Not only was I jealous of how easily he woke and jumped out of bed, but I was also missing feeling his morning wood that only seconds ago had been bumping up against my leg. I quickly forgot about my loss because I got a new treat: the sight of Ben walking away from me. And let me tell you, Ben had an ass that could inspire men to write poetry. The previous day I'd only caught a quick glimpse of it, but today I was getting the full picture. Damn!

It was almost painful to see the man pull his shorts on. He was out the door and into the bathroom and was back in remarkably short time, showered and looking entirely too perky for such an early hour.

"Shower's yours," he told me as he dressed.

Maybe the shower would help me to wake up now that Ben's naked body was no longer a carrot in front of me to get me moving. It took me longer than Ben to shower, even though I had less body to wash than he did. The man seemed to be a morning person—this could be a problem.

Ben was waiting for me in his room. As soon as I closed the door to get dressed, Ben was on me—or more precisely, Ben's lips were on me. For someone who hadn't kissed a guy before yesterday, he sure took to it like a duck to water.

He slipped his hand under the waistband of my shorts, cupping my balls and then moving upward to gently caress my erection.

"Wish I had time to help you with that," he said with a smile.

"Hey! You got me high and dry here and you're just going to walk away?"

"Have to. Time to get to work."

"There's work to be done here," I told him, shaking my erection at him.

After a chuckle, Ben turned serious. Oh, no, this wasn't going to be good, whatever it was.

"So I've been thinking," he started. My heart rate automatically increased, adrenaline seeping into my system. Was this going to be where he told me that yesterday and last night had been a mistake?

"I haven't been super friendly to you so far this summer."

"Ya think?" I asked, feeling a bit of snarkiness was due.

"Yes. And if that suddenly changes now, people could get suspicious."

"You mean your mom and my dad."

"Yes. We don't usually see anybody else."

"Okay. So what do we do about it?" I asked him.

"I think when we're with them or within sight of them, we have to continue to act like we don't like each other. I'm going to have to continue to be a real prick to you, and you're going to have to continue to act all surly-like. Think you can do that?"

"What do you mean 'surly-like'?"

Ben wasn't a man to pull his punches. "You haven't wanted to be here. You've been pissy about that all summer. You can't deny that."

I huffed. "Fine. Right. Okay. Maybe I haven't been super nice. But…."

"I know. Extenuating circumstances and all that shit. All I'm saying is we have to continue to play those parts, even though there's…."

"Even though there's… what? Something more, I hope."

Ben looked down at his feet for a moment and then looked back up to meet my gaze. "Yes, I hope so too. I like you—now—and I like what we did last night. I want to do more of that and a whole lot more—with you."

With words like that, it was inevitable that I was going to smile.

Further conversation would have to wait, though, because we both heard Ben's mother calling us down for breakfast. I threw the last of my clothes on really fast, and we went down the stairs together.

Melinda smiled at me with a positively cheery, "Good morning." Sheesh, both mother and son were morning people. I knew that, but having it reiterated so early in the day made it more effective.

"Morning."

"You feeling better today? Get some good sleep last night?"

"I slept really well. Thanks."

"You look a lot better today."

"I'm feeling better. Not quite as worn-out as I was last night."

As we ate Melinda's hearty farm breakfast that would fuel us for a morning of hard farm work, she asked her son, "What are you working on today?"

"Once I finish with morning chores, I want to do some more work on that fence between us and the Henderson farm. It's been falling down, but I couldn't do much without some help. What's his name can help," he said, gesturing at me without looking at me.

"Oh, goodie," I muttered, continuing to act my part.

"Doesn't look like he's worth much, but at least he can help hold stuff while I do the work."

"Be nice," his mother cautioned, casting a quick glance my way.

Since we were trying to keep everyone in the dark about our relationship being anything other than hostile, I decided to goad him a little, so I echoed her words, "Yeah, be nice."

"Whatever," he muttered as he finished his breakfast. When his mother's back was turned, he gave me a quick smile before finishing his breakfast. I was still eating, but when Ben was ready, he said, "Come on, city slacker. Work to be done."

"I'm still eating," I complained, which wasn't an act. I really was still eating, and I wasn't ready to leave yet.

"Tough. We're burning daylight. Time to start work. You'll learn to eat faster or you'll be hungry." And he had the audacity to take my plate away from me and put it on the kitchen counter. "I said it's time to start work." Ben really did play a convincing dick.

I might have called him something like "prick," and he might have told me I was lazy. It felt natural, so I hoped his mother didn't suspect that we'd spent the previous night getting physically intimate with each other.

Because of our late night activities, not to mention almost dying during the day, I was not my most perky that morning. It was true that I was feeling better, but I was still not 100 percent back, so it wasn't too difficult for me to complain and egg Ben on just a bit.

"Stop being such a fucking prima donna," Ben told me, which earned him my own retort.

"Bite me, farm boy."

"Just shut up and get to work."

By that point we were well clear of the house and of anyone who might be able to hear our conversation, so we felt it was safe to talk.

# Chapter Eleven
# A Break at the Swimming Hole

AFTER OUR morning chores, Ben and I rode one of the ATVs out to a distant part of the farm where the fence needed to be repaired. When we got there, it appeared that either cows from a neighbor's pasture had knocked the fence down and come across to help themselves to something to eat in the field, or the fence had fallen down and the cows were opportunistic. However it had happened, the fence was down, and the crops for a good twenty-five to thirty feet were either trampled or chewed down to the ground.

Ben cursed a good deal at the neighbors, the neighbors' cows, cows in general, the sun, the age of the fence, and anything else he could think of to curse about. After working with the man for six weeks, I'd learned to tune out a lot of his running colorful commentary. My best guess was that his father had done the same thing, and working with his dad, Ben had just picked up the habit. I could be wrong, but I doubted it.

Of course it didn't help that the sky was crystal clear, so we had no cloud cover to keep the heat down. The sun was blazing, intent on baking the ground and everything anywhere out in the open. We both had quickly stripped out of our shirts early on, but even with that, we were sweating a good deal. It was hard work digging better holes for fence posts, lugging heavy rocks to keep them in place, and then restringing the barbed wire from post to post. It didn't help that we had to do a lot of extra shoveling in one place where the cows had trampled a rut. But we did it.

At noon when we finished, I simply sat down on the ground and fell backward, groaning with relief that I was off my feet for a few minutes. The sun was still blazing high in the sky, and the ground on which I was lying was hot, but it felt good for a moment. Ben had a couple of bottles of water, both of which were very warm, any chill they might once have possessed long gone. He forewarned me, but it was still a surprise when he dribbled some of the water from one bottle onto me. Hot water on a hot body on a hot day just didn't help, so I asked him to stop.

"How far is that swimming hole we were at yesterday?" I asked him. I'd worked there for six weeks, but their farm was huge, and I wasn't the world's best navigator, even under the best of circumstances.

"Completely in another direction," he told me. "Let's go back to the house and eat lunch, and then I'll see if I can find an excuse to get us back over there."

When we got back, the house was surprisingly quiet. Nothing was locked up, but it was empty. Ben's mother had gone to town to shop, leaving him a note and lunch. When I spied the words on the paper in his hands, I said, "Cool."

"So," he asked, "do you want to stay here, or go out to the swimming hole?"

"Swimming hole," I answered quickly and decisively. I suddenly hesitated. "Does anyone else from neighboring farms ever use it?"

"No. The pool is spring fed from springs on our farm, and no one else is supposed to be there unless we invite them. I suspect most people have something similar on their own farms. Besides, I don't think any of them even know about ours."

"So we're safe if we... do stuff there?"

He gave me a goofy smile and asked, "You want to do stuff?"

"I want to do stuff," I told him, mirroring his smile and his giddiness.

Last night had been nice, but we'd been trying to keep it quiet, so all we did was kiss a lot and feel each other up. I had licked parts of Ben's chest enough to see that he responded well, but that's the last I remember, so I suspect I fell asleep in midlick. Yesterday had been a tough day.

Lunch that day was consumed in record speed. Ben dashed up to his room really fast, and less than a minute later, we were back on the three-wheeler and headed toward the swimming hole. I had no idea how big their farm was in farm terms or acreage or whatever scale a farmer would use. But it was big. We were not able to just drive flat out—there were no roads, just lanes, and in places they were little more than trails. If we could have just flown, it wouldn't have been more than three or four minutes, but it took us nearly ten minutes to get there. But I wasn't complaining because I was sitting behind Ben with my arms wrapped around his naked, tanned, sweaty torso.

I don't know if it was appropriate or not, but rather than just hold on to him, my hands were gently but brazenly toying with his nipples. I was getting positive feedback from Ben—at least I assumed that him slowing the vehicle down, tossing his head back, and moaning was positive feedback—so I continued. Or maybe it would be more accurate to say that I didn't stop, because in point of fact, I didn't think I could have stopped if I needed to. There was something about the feel of Ben's body beneath my touch that ignited a fire inside me, a fire that, once started, threatened to burn uncontrollably.

We came upon the stream before I realized we were there. I hadn't really been able to pay attention the last time I'd been there—first because I'd been unconscious from heat exhaustion and the second time from nearly drowning. Today, though, I could appreciate the privacy the place afforded us. The spring came above ground at the bottom of a small hill. The waters from the spring collected in a small pool. A number of trees had seeded over the years and taken root alongside the small pool of tranquil water, creating a beautiful pastoral setting.

Back amid the trees, the shade and the coolness of the water created a little sanctuary from the heat and humidity of the rest of the world. It was official—I was in love with Ben's little hidden oasis on their land. From inside the little copse of trees around the natural pool, I realized we were able to see the most likely path someone would have to take were they to come in search of us.

As someone who had clearly been to the pool countless times over the years, Ben stripped off his shorts almost as soon as we were under the cover of the trees. He lost them so quickly I half wondered if he was planning to just fling them off and let them fall wherever they might land. I was grateful to see that he didn't do that. He kept hold of them, and once we were by the water, he put them within reach but also back from the water.

As I walked behind Ben, I marveled at the man's exquisite body, particularly his beautiful backside. It took a lot to rival Ben's front side, but it happened. Regardless of which way he was, going or coming, Ben made an impressive figure.

All over again, I was flabbergasted by the fact that I was about to get naked with a man who just a short time ago seemed to hate my guts. And even though he was getting free labor out of me, he'd still treated me like a major imposition and something to be endured, like his own personal cross to bear. Now, thankfully, that was but a memory.

When he reached the edge of the small pool, Ben stopped, dipped one foot into the water even though he likely already knew what the water would feel like, and turned back toward me. And rather than be confronted by the surly, angry countenance of a man who seemed to hate the fact that I was even breathing the same air as him, Ben now looked positively radiant, delighted to see me.

And if I hadn't been able to tell from his face, I had all the confirmation I needed from looking at a better barometer—his dick. Not only did Ben gaze back toward me, giving me a smoldering hot look, but his dick quickly started to rise when he had me in sight. I had never seen that response in any man before, and I had to say—I liked it. Ben was responding physically to me, to my presence, in terms that I found affirming and uplifting for my self-esteem, which had taken such a major beating that summer.

What red-blooded American gay man wouldn't feel good to see a hunk like Ben pop an instant woodie just by looking his way? I know I wasn't upset by his reaction. Hell no. I liked it, I loved it, and I wanted to wrap my hands around it, followed by the rest of my body.

Since I'd been so wiped out last night, we hadn't done much beyond just kiss and caress. It was quickly clear to me that Ben was ready for more—far more—and I was most eager to give him what he wanted. Ben dropped to his knees in front of me with an adoring look that made my heart feel like it was going to pound right out of my chest at any minute. He helped me slip out of my clothes until I was as naked—and as erect—as he was. I wanted to drop to my knees as well, but before I could do that, Ben had his hands on my hips holding me upright.

Ben's eyes were inches from my crotch. He was studying my erection like a man seeing one for the first time. There was a look of wonder on his face that I found intriguing. When he didn't move his eyes away after a moment, I had to ask, "Is something wrong? Do I have mud on my dick or something like that?"

"No. There is nothing wrong—absolutely nothing at all."

Not buying it, I tried to dig into his reaction to figure out what he wasn't saying. "You have seen a dick before. After all, you've got one of your own, so what is it?"

He gazed up at me with a look of pure wonder. "Yes, I've got one of my own, but I've never seen another guy get hard before. And I like it."

"You've... never been with anyone else?"

"I didn't say that," he clarified. Too bad I wasn't any clearer now than I had been before.

"Huh?" I asked. "I don't understand."

"Think about it. I've never seen another guy's dick get hard. But...." He looked at me as if I should understand what he was talking about. And then it hit me.

"Oh fuck," I practically shouted, which made him automatically look around just to be absolutely sure we were all alone and no one was lurking nearby. "You've had sex with a woman."

"Um... well... maybe kind of."

"I don't want to think about such things," I told him. "I'm here. You're here. We're both naked. There are better things to do." And just to prove my point, I pushed him back so he was lying flat on his back. I dropped to my knees beside him and demonstrated one of the things we could do that was better.

I decided to move quickly so he wouldn't have time to complain or to hesitate or do something stupid. Before he could form words, I had my lips wrapped around the head of his dick. I tried to keep an eye on his face while also teasing the head of his dick with my tongue. It was cute the way his back arched up and his eyes rolled back in his head. Even though I was making this up as I went, clearly I was doing okay with my improvisation.

For the next ten minutes, I used my hands and my tongue to explore his erection and to almost worship the tall, slender shaft. I traced the veins along the underside of his erection, tangled my tongue in his pubic hair at the base, and toyed with the slit in the head at the top. I was everywhere, not wanting to miss a single inch.

When I had him slicked up pretty well, I decided it was time to try taking some of him into my throat. I'd read stories about guys doing this, and it sounded so freaking hot. Well, I gave it a shot, and I did okay, but I needed more practice—lots more practice. But the good news was that Ben was most likely willing to let me practice on him.

I know I did something right, because Ben got so worked up he came. And not just that—he erupted. The first shot went way over his head, landing on the grass beyond his head. It was freaking awesome to watch, and only after it was over did I realize I could have (probably should have) let him cum in my mouth. Oh, well, that was something to try another time. And I knew there would be another time. Absolutely.

Ben was so relaxed after that he actually dozed off. I was pleased I could do that to him and for him, but I was also a little annoyed because he was all mellow, but I was still hard up and just as horny as he'd been a few minutes ago. I wanted to shake him awake and tell him, "Dude! Me too," but I didn't. I let him sleep for a few minutes.

I didn't sleep but instead lay on the grass beside Ben and watched him sleep. It was so peaceful to watch his chest rising and falling as he breathed. I had the most overwhelming urge to lean forward and lick his nipple closest to me, but I was good and let him sleep.

About twenty minutes later, Ben was still sleeping while I lay on the grass in the shade contemplating the universe. I thought I heard an engine of some sort way off in the distance. I couldn't be sure. I wasn't going to take any chances, so I got up, found my clothes, and pulled them back on.

When I heard the same sound again, I decided to wake Ben to see if he knew what it was.

"Ben! Wake up. I thought I heard something." The poor guy went from sound asleep to fully awake and on high alert in just a matter of seconds.

"What?" he asked, trying to get up to speed. "What'd you hear?"

"I thought I heard something like an engine. I'm not sure. Would anyone else drive here?"

"No. Well, maybe." Ben pulled on his shorts. I swear I almost felt physical pain at the sight of him covering his beautiful body. I so loved looking at Ben's naked body that the idea of covering him with clothes just seemed wrong—completely wrong. But we couldn't take any chances of being found in a compromising position or circumstance.

Once he was dressed, Ben listened and thought he heard something too, but he wasn't any more able to identify the source of the sound than I had been.

"We better get back to work," he told me. I didn't want to, but I couldn't argue. If someone was out there somewhere, if they came upon us working, it would look more natural or convincing than if we were lying naked by the watering hole—well, natural to them, not to me.

In the end, we never did figure out the source of the engine sound that afternoon, and we never did see anyone the rest of the afternoon. We worked on little odd jobs around the farm throughout the remainder of the day without seeing anyone and without anyone coming to visit us or check on us. No one ever did. Even my dad didn't bother to check up on me. I guess he thought Ben was enough of a man, a man's man, that he could trust Ben to keep me in line and out of trouble. If he only knew. I was actually quite glad he didn't. The longer he didn't know anything, the better for me.

# Chapter Twelve
# Making Love

WHILE I would have loved to spend another night in bed with Ben, cuddled together despite the heat and humidity, I couldn't get away with that two nights in a row, so I had to return to my father's old farmhouse to sleep that night. It was hot, it was humid, it was disgustingly miserable, which made sleep next to impossible. Also, the bed I was sleeping in was much less comfortable than Ben's bed had been the previous night. Still, I did sleep at least a few hours.

It was weird that just the time of the day when the temperature was most conducive for sleep was the time farmers got out of bed. It didn't make sense to me, but I didn't get a vote in how farmers decided things, so I got up when the alarm went off the next morning and hauled my sleepy self over to Ben's farm to begin work.

While I was working all day every day, I didn't know what my father was doing. I was vaguely curious, but I didn't want to spend any more time with him than I had to, so I didn't ask. All I knew was that he drove off somewhere every day for a few hours. He could have been going to the local mall for all I knew. He didn't offer and I didn't ask. The less I saw him, the less he could stick his nose into my life. He'd fucked up my life enough the last time. I was determined to not give him another chance to do that again, and the less time I spent with him, the less opportunity he had to do something awful.

I was cordial when our paths crossed, but I worked very hard to minimize the number of times our paths crossed in any given day. It wasn't hard in the morning because I had to be up and out of the house before dawn each day to get over next door to get to work. My father was definitely not a morning person, so he wasn't awake when I left each morning. Who knew how late he slept each day. I did know that he stayed up significantly later than I did each night, because occasionally I'd wake up and hear the television still on quite late at night.

So what he did to occupy his time was a mystery to me, and I was satisfied to leave him his mysteries. I just wanted him to return the favor and let me have mine. I don't think he was taking to country living any better than I was. The major difference was that I had something to occupy my every waking moment, where he had who knew what?

We'd been there for a couple of months when my dad started to make trips back to the city to do some work in his office. As much as I missed the city and my friends and my old room, my bed, and any of a number of things, I was glad to see him drive away.

The city was a long drive from the farm, so whenever he made that trip he always spent the night. I loved those days each week when he was gone. The first time he was gone, I observed. The second time, I plotted. The third week, I had Ben primed and ready. The instant our work was done, we hightailed it over to my house and shed our clothes as we made our way to my bedroom. We had intended to just get naked and do wild things to one another. But we quickly discovered that after a full day of working and sweating, we were both too disgusting to lick or even touch, so we had to take quick showers before we could really get down to business. And what business we had.

I never tired of seeing Ben's naked body, especially when it was topped off by his penis standing up at full mast. The man had a body that made me salivate. The first time we were together naked, I was on my knees in front of him in a heartbeat, practicing my oral skills. I thought I was getting better, and apparently so did Ben's penis, because he was fairly quickly pushing me away and holding me at arm's length with a pained look on his face.

"What's wrong?" I asked him, confused.

"Just a minute."

"What?"

"You got me too close."

"That's kind of the whole idea," I told him.

"Fine, but I'd like it to last just a little bit longer."

"Okay. What do we do while we wait?"

Ben used his bigger body and greater strength to lift me up and stand me back on my feet so he could drop down in front of me and attempt to copy my earlier moves. Either Ben was a very good student, had some natural ability, or he'd done this before. He swore later that it was just natural ability. All I knew is that he swallowed my dick and used his throat muscles to do things to me that I'd never felt before.

And then it was my turn to be brought to the edge. The only problem was that I couldn't get him off my dick fast enough, so I was getting all weak-kneed before I knew what hit me. Ben helped me to my bed after that and laid me on my back, crawling up on top of my ultrarelaxed body.

As Ben held himself just above my body and looked down into my eyes from his position above me, I think part of me melted. Ben's eyes were smoldering hot. I swear I was looking deep into his very being. I knew that wasn't true, but there was such a depth, such an intensity to his stare, it felt like that was the case.

"You are so frigging hot," he told me as he slowly lowered his lips to mine.

"You too," I told him when we took a break to breathe.

Ben was holding himself slightly apart from me, but I wasn't having any of that. I wrapped my arms around his torso and pulled him down onto my body. I wanted to feel his skin make contact with mine everywhere possible. I wanted to feel his weight on top of me, pressing me down into the mattress. I wanted to feel his hands in my hair, and not see them holding his body up and away from mine. Ben seemed to have no argument when I showed him what I wanted.

Even though he'd just blown me—very well, too, I might add—feeling his hard body pressed against mine had me hard again in no time. I wasn't the only one. Our two dicks were like dueling warriors between our bellies, each jostling the other. There was friction, which felt exquisite.

Apparently that friction was doing things for Ben, because he suddenly stiffened and whimpered before he pulled his mouth from mine and cried out. I felt the reason for his cry as there was a sudden wetness between us. Ben shuddered one final time before he collapsed on top of me, resting his head on my shoulder.

"I can feel your heart beating," he hoarsely whispered to me. "I hear it too. Wow. That's amazing." The awe in his voice was clearly detectable.

"You're what's making it beat so hard," I told him.

Ben was quiet for a moment before he whispered, "I never thought I'd have a chance to feel like this about another guy."

I kissed the top of his head, since I didn't know what to say that was equal to his statement. Anything I might have said would just be inadequate, so other than the kiss I kept my mouth shut (for once).

I would have given just about anything to have Ben in my bed all night long. The thought of going to sleep curled up around him and waking up the next morning with him wrapped around me was just about the hottest thing I could imagine. Someday. Someday it would happen. But we both knew that we couldn't take that risk right now. No matter how much we both wanted it, we couldn't risk it. So, with great reluctance Ben crawled back out of my bed a few hours after he'd arrived, and found his clothes so he could get dressed. Just inside the front door I hugged him and didn't want to let him go. Finally, though, Ben was the stronger of the two of us and pulled away from me, slipping out the door quickly so he couldn't change his mind.

It was so bizarre, but after an experience that felt so awesome—being in bed with Ben—going back to my empty bed was just painful. Each time he left, I threw myself back onto my bed and tried to find his scent. Every week it was so abundantly clear to me that Ben had been in my bed. He had the most incredible masculine smell, and it gave me such great joy to know that he'd been in my bed, at least for a while.

My dad typically didn't get back until quite late the day after he left for New York City. If we'd been really gutsy, we would have taken another chance to spend some time together in my bed, but we didn't dare. Surely if we did, that would be the week he'd come back early and would walk in to find me in bed with yet another guy. And knowing what Ben and I were like when we were alone in my bedroom, we'd both be naked and as hard as granite.

The next time Ben was in my bed, we did more than we had been able to the previous week. We hadn't talked about it, but I was determined that I was going to have Ben more a part of me than he had been before. Little did I know that he had made a similar vow to himself, only with the tables turned. So, he wanted me in him, and I wanted him in me. What were we to do? Simple, we had to do each other—so we did.

That evening while we had the house to ourselves, we spent three hours in bed together learning more new things about each other. I learned that when I slid inside Ben, his eyelids fluttered and his mouth slowly opened and stayed that way. It was so incredible to be together with him, but to be joined together in such an intimate fashion was truly magical for both of us. I knew it was for me, and it sure looked that way for Ben too.

Once I was all the way inside him, it was so hard to know what to do. Part of me wanted to just brace myself and look down at his gorgeous features and to see what I was doing to him. But the instinct to move was equally strong and left me wanting both—at the same time.

To move or not to move? That was the question. That first time we made love was so incredible that I shed some tears. I wept softly because it felt so fucking incredible to be joined with him and to know that I was the first man he'd ever allowed to do this with him. To feel the sensations on my dick was nice, but that was only about 5 percent of what I was feeling. The vast bulk of what I was feeling was emotional. We were sharing something so personal, so intimate, so magical. I knew people did it millions of times every day, but we didn't. We'd never done it before, with each other or with anyone else. This was a first for both of us, and it was so incredible that all I could do was shed a few tears in joy.

Half an hour later, when we had reversed positions and I was on my back with Ben on me, giving me a brand-new experience, he understood why I'd reacted the way I had when I'd been where he was now. It was one of the most over-the-top experiences of my life. I wanted to shout from the roof that I was together with a man who was growing into such an amazingly important part in my life. I'd never felt about another man the way I was coming to feel about Ben. I didn't dare to say the words that I felt out loud. I was so afraid that if I said what I was feeling I would send him running in fear, and I didn't want to risk that happening.

That night when Ben had to leave, it hurt way more than it had the previous week when he left. I knew he felt it too. It only took one look at his face to see that. Standing there at the door that night, looking at him clearly feeling so sad that we had to be apart, I wanted to just grab him by the hand and run away with him somewhere where we could be together without having to worry about what others might think, without having to wonder if someone was going to see us, and without having to keep a constantly vigilant eye over the other's shoulder. The concept of being able to devote all of our attention to each other like straight couples was something we couldn't even dream about having.

# Chapter Thirteen
# Dinner Date

THE MORNING after we'd first made love, I was concerned because Ben was quiet. He was always more reserved than I was, but that morning he was even more so than usual. At first I didn't push him, partly because I didn't know what was going on inside his head, and I didn't have the slightest clue how to go about asking him what he was thinking. Even more than that, I was afraid that I'd find the words to ask him what he was thinking and feeling, and he'd tell me something awful like it had been a mistake and he wished we hadn't done it or something horrible like that. I was feeling so fragile after an hour that I thought I was going to break into a thousand tiny pieces, each hurting as much as the bigger whole felt.

It was brutally hot that day, on top of everything else, so we had to take breaks periodically as we worked on fences or weeding or whatever the hell we were doing. It didn't matter because whatever it was, it was all in the background for me. I was working on autopilot. All of my thoughts were on Ben and how I loved him. There! I'd thought the words. I expected the sky to fall now because I'd had the audacity to think it.

It was midmorning, and we were sitting in what shade we could find, both quiet. When Ben spoke, I was surprised, but probably not as surprised as he was by my answer to his question. His question was simple—"You okay?"

And my answer? I don't know why I said it, but my answer to Ben was "I love you."

There, I'd said it. The words were out there. My heart was nearly bursting with the way I was feeling, and I had to say it or it was gonna just pop out of me in some uncontrolled way.

"What?" he asked quietly.

I was committed. I'd said it, so there was no pretending I hadn't. "I love you," I repeated.

And that was all it took. Right there in the middle of that field of corn standing tall above our heads, Ben threw himself at me, and I suddenly had two arms full of the best man in the world. I'd cried when we'd made love the previous night, but today was Ben's turn. Right there in that field, Ben wrapped around me, and I heard him weeping quietly. He was trying to hide it, but that wasn't possible.

"I love you," he said to me, and I swear I levitated right there. The man I had just told I loved had just done me the honor of saying the words back to me. And it didn't feel like he said it to be even. He said it because I'd somehow lifted the burden from the situation and allowed him to say what he was really feeling. Without having that conversation, I was reading into his reaction that he was relieved that I'd taken the first step so he could say what he wanted to, that he loved me too. Who could ask for a better moment than the one we were having that morning in the middle of the cornfield? We could have had a better place to have that moment—anyplace with air-conditioning would have been great—but we had each other, and who could ask for anything more?

"Really?" Ben whispered to me.

"You bet your boots, cowboy," I told him.

"Hey! I'm no cowboy. What's this cowboy shit?" he teased me.

"I don't know. It just popped out, kind of like me telling you that I loved you."

"I'm glad that popped out. I've been thinking all morning how the hell I was going to work up the nerve to say those same words to you."

"Really?"

"Yes."

"I've been so terrified all morning that you were regretting what we did last night and were looking for some way to let me down and tell me it was a big mistake."

"Not on your life," he told me as he held me close.

For the rest of that day as we worked on fences and fields and a dozen other chores, we both kept checking to be sure we were alone before we repeated the words to each other. "I love you." It was a great day—they just didn't get any better than that day.

By that point it was a good thing we weren't trying to act like we still hated each other, because I don't think I could have pulled that off. Over the weeks we'd moved from acting mad at one another to being a bit surly, and then to quasi cordial, and finally to almost friendly.

Melinda had invited me and my dad to have dinner with her and Ben that night, so just when I was feeling a constant urge to throw him to the ground and kiss the stuffing out of him, my dad was going to be there, which was a total mood killer.

Playing games had been hard. We were both so fucking sick of playing the games straight society required of us. Why couldn't we be ourselves? We weren't hurting anyone, so why couldn't everyone fuck off and let us have our moment of happiness? We didn't want much— just to be left alone to be in love. Was that too much to ask? Given my dad's track record, I already knew the answer to that question.

We were both tired that night so we were quiet through the meal. After dinner, while my dad and Melinda had iced tea on the front porch, Ben and I cleaned up the dishes and talked quietly. We didn't say a lot of words out loud. We did a lot of talking with our eyes and our smiles. I was doing the dishes next to the man who'd told me that he loved me. Me! I'd take what I could get because what I had was the love of the best man I'd ever known.

When we were alone, we'd whisper back and forth to each other, looking over our shoulders to make sure our parents were still occupied outside. I was washing. Each time I finished a dish and passed it to him to rinse and dry, I'd whisper, "I love you, Ben," or some variation on those words. He did the same, eventually growing bold enough to even lean in and kiss me occasionally when words alone would not do.

One of the benefits—if there were any—of living in an old house was that the floors were all squeaky, so you couldn't move anywhere without some floorboards making noise. We used that to our benefit that night. While my dad and his mom were busy talking about something out front, once we finished the dishes, we moved into a sheltered spot in the kitchen. With the lights turned off, we were able to wrap our arms around each other and kiss, trying to crawl inside each other.

We were getting into it so much that I even put my back against the wall, pulled Ben close and wrapped my legs around his body with him holding me up while we kissed. I had a slab of granite in my pants, and Ben did too. I wanted to drop to my knees and take care of that for him but we didn't dare to even think about that. I wanted to go upstairs to his bedroom and his supercomfortable bed and make slow love to the man who loved me—the man I loved—but we couldn't do that.

When we heard the floors start to squeak in the living room, we separated fast and each took a seat at the kitchen table, trying to look innocent.

Melinda appeared in the kitchen doorway.

"It's awfully quiet in here. Just checking to see if you two killed each other yet or what."

"Nah," Ben told her. "Too tired. Long day today."

I looked up at her and smiled and said, "Fantastic dinner, Melinda, as always. Your cooking is the best I've ever had. I wish you could teach my dad how to cook."

She snickered. "I've heard you say that before. If I remember right, you said he's not gonna win any prizes for his cooking."

"You can say that again," I told her.

I was having breakfast at their house every morning. Lunch was again something she prepared for us to eat at midday. But dinner, well, dinner I had to eat at my own house. Let's say that dinner was not the high point of my day. At first when we moved here, dinner was something to be dreaded or endured. But then my dad discovered frozen foods that he could reheat in the microwave, so we started to have those. That made dinner bearable, but I still looked forward to our once a week dinner at Melinda and Ben's house.

My dad popped up behind Melinda and asked, "So, is there blood on the floor yet in here?"

"Nope," she told him. "Just two tired farmers."

"Hard work'll do that," he commented. I wanted to ask how he knew anything about that, but I held my tongue. I couldn't hold Ben's hand like I wanted, but I did manage to hold my tongue. "Time to go home, Adam. It's getting dark."

I could remember a time when the arrival of night was the signal for me to go out and meet my friends and go have fun. Now the arrival of darkness was simply an indication that it was time to go to bed. How much my life had changed.

# Chapter Fourteen
# The Random Wrath of
# Mother Nature

THAT AUGUST we had more oppressive heat, but we also had some of the most intensive thunderstorms I think I've ever witnessed in my entire life. I didn't know it was possible for thunder to be as loud as what I heard those hot summer afternoons.

I'd noticed that Ben always kept an eye on the skies those days, and any time the sky got dark and remotely threatening, he insisted that we head to the barn. At first I didn't understand, but after my first country summer thunderstorm with all of its lightning and thunder, I finally got it.

When one of those storms hit, you absolutely did not want to be caught out in the field without cover from the lighting. The day after the first storm, Ben showed me a tree that had been hit by lightning the previous summer. I could not believe what he was showing me. It was as if the lightning bolt had just reached down from the sky and wrapped itself around this gigantic tree. There were clear burn marks all around the tree from the top all the way to the bottom.

The lightning strike had killed the tree, so no leaves were there to get in the way of seeing what I'd never seen before. I could almost picture the lightning sizzling as it enveloped the tree, cooking the juices inside its core as the temperature jumped from whatever it had been by several thousand degrees in the span of a second. That first storm and the sight of that tree, and I was a complete convert. I instantly had a healthy respect for Mother Nature and joined Ben from that point forward in keeping an eye on the sky. Whenever there were dark clouds building on the horizon, we hightailed it back to the barn to wait it out to see if this would be a quick little storm or, as Ben called it, a gully washer.

On days when the weather was sort of constantly threatening or plain rainy all day, we spent our time working at the roadside stand, giving Ben's mom time off to do some of the other things she needed to do. We didn't always have a lot to do there. It all depended on how much business we got and how much restocking we needed to do or how much cleaning we needed to do.

We busied ourselves by sorting through the produce and fruit that was on display, picking out the less than perfect stuff and setting it aside to sell at a lower price. Melinda liked everything to look perfect, pristine. She said that was what made people buy, so I didn't argue. She'd built a prosperous market and clearly knew what she was talking about.

Business was slower on rainy days, but we still had a fairly steady stream of customers. The only part of rainy days I hated was when someone would come to the stand and buy a big quantity of something, like a bushel of apples. Why did I hate that? Simple. I was the one who had to carry the bushel basket of apples to their car and put it in their trunk or wherever they wanted it.

Nine times out of ten, it was someone who didn't think to unlock the car before stepping out into the rain. All it took most of them was to push a button on their key fob, but most of them didn't do that until they got to their car, like it was some big surprise that they had to unlock it before they could open the door or the trunk. The ones I hated the most were the people who got up to their car and then suddenly remembered, but then had to stop and search for their keys in their pockets and purses.

Those times, I got soaked. By the time I got the produce loaded and ran back inside the store, I was dripping wet, my clothes soaked, my hair plastered to my head. The only thing that made those times bearable was when a customer was nice enough to slip me a couple of dollars as thanks for helping get their purchases to their car.

Those tips were about the only source of money I had, and I safeguarded that cash like my life depended on it. Those tips were why I was always willing to help carry stuff. Not everyone thought to do it, but when they did, I was glad to take it and sock it away once I got home. I hated being poor, and being stuck in the middle of nowhere with no money made me feel trapped and isolated, even with Ben. Having a few dollars tucked away made it better.

Sometimes when we worked there—Ben ran the cash register and I floated around doing a bunch of different things—I would tease Ben by commenting on how hot some customer had been. Many of the customers were mothers who brought their teenaged sons along with them. Those times meant that I wouldn't get to carry things for them and I wouldn't get a tip, but sometimes the sons they brought were beautiful and gave Ben and me something to look at. After they left, I'd tell Ben something like, "Wasn't he hot? Damn." He'd scowl at me. I wasn't saying I wanted to mount the guy in the driveway, I was just saying that the guy was worth looking at and had a nice body.

Sometimes Ben knew the teens who accompanied their parents and was able to say hi to them in that quiet, retiring country manner where two words made an entire conversation. I always liked watching Ben interact with guys he obviously knew. Sometimes they traded a few more words, and that was always fascinating to watch. Ben was basically a man of few words, so anytime he shared some of those words I paid close attention.

But sometimes those teens pissed me off too. I especially hated the mothers who brought their teenaged daughters with them. Not all of them, but those who knew Ben, because they would often flirt shamelessly with him. When that happened, I felt myself stand up straighter. I wanted to march over and shove them back and say, "Mine." But of course I couldn't do that, so I had to stand there and watch and feel like crap because I couldn't say anything.

It was hard to watch some of them because they were sometimes really aggressive, especially those that felt the need to touch Ben—a simple hand resting on his bare arm, a touch to his back. One even had the audacity to pat him on the ass when he leaned over to reach for something. He was startled by that one, which only seemed to amuse the girl. I was ready to walk over and break her arms off, but I couldn't do that.

Sometimes what I did was walk over and stand beside Ben behind the counter where he was working. I didn't say anything those times, but I stood there and was just a presence. That seemed to make them stop being so grabby, so I considered my work done when that happened. None of them knew me, and I was happy with that, because it made me a bit of a man of mystery.

All of the rain that August and the heat we'd been experiencing all summer made for bumper crops of just about everything they had growing. When it didn't rain we traipsed through the mud of the fields to pick corn, hauling bushels of the stuff to the market where it sold faster than seemed possible. We didn't pick it all at once but picked a couple of days' worth, storing some of it in the walk-in cooler at the stand.

I learned that summer that tomatoes are fucking heavy. The days we picked them were tough because they weighed a ton and hauling them around was hard work. We also had to be careful with them because they bruised really easily and bruises made them unsellable.

The first of their apples were ready to start picking in late August. Apples weighed a ton as well, but at least Ben drove a tractor out into the orchard on those days, with a big flatbed trailer behind it to haul everything back to the stand. Still, we had to fill the baskets and haul them to the trailer—and then unload them down at the stand, so we still had to work; it was just a different sort of work.

# Chapter Fifteen
# Late August

IT WAS late August when I learned something about Ben that surprised me. Despite knowing him rather well—including biblically, I might add—still a great many things about the man were unknown to me. I learned a whopper when yet another mother and daughter arrived to do some shopping at the stand. While the mother picked over fruit and produce, the daughter sidled up to Ben and batted her eyelashes. Clearly Ben knew this one, and she knew him. How, I didn't know. I moved closer to listen to whatever they were saying as discreetly as I could.

"So, school begins in a couple of weeks. You ready? Oh, wait, you quit, didn't you?" she said to him. I couldn't tell if she honestly had forgotten or she was trying to inflict some anguish on him. Wait a minute. Quit? Ben had quit school? What was this all about? Oh, wait, now I remembered Melinda telling me something about that way back when we'd first arrived, back when I didn't care what Ben did or didn't do.

"Yeah, I did. But I'm thinking about it."

"You better come back," she ordered him. "This is our senior year, so it's going to be awesome. We'll own that school this year. And you know there are all those senior dances. We'll go together, and you could give me that dance you've been promising me forever. I can see it now, you all done up in a tux and me in that beautiful little black dress I've had waiting to wear to a dance. Think about it, Benjamin. We're gonna look so fucking hot together, you all tall and handsome and me all sexy and shapely and stunning. We're gonna have all of 'em watching us, wanting to be us, or wanting to be with us." I swear that she squealed at that point. I don't think I'd ever heard a person squeal before, but she did. "It's gonna be so great. We are gonna be the power couple of that school. I just know it. You and me are gonna fucking rule that place."

I wanted to ask Ben as soon as she was gone about the whole thing, but wouldn't you know that we had one customer after another that morning, and I couldn't get a minute alone to ask him until more than an hour later. When I did, believe me, I wasted no time in asking, "What the fuck was up with that girl this morning?"

"What girl?" he asked, like he didn't know what I was talking about. Did he?

"That girl who got so close to you it looked like she wanted to crawl into your pants pocket. The one who talked about you owing her a dance."

Ben looked down. Not a good sign. "Oh, her. That's Amelia. She and I…."

"Yes?" I asked when he didn't automatically continue. "You what?" I asked. He still hadn't looked up. "Ben?"

"We kind of dated for a while," he explained, speaking quickly.

"Okay. Dates like in going out for dinner and a movie?"

"Yeah, something like that."

And then it hit me. "Did you sleep with her?"

Ben wouldn't look up. He remained silent. I had my answer. He might have expected me to be angry, but I was mostly feeling sorry for him. If I was angry, I was pissed off about that and not at Ben.

"Yeah," he said softly. I put my arm around him since we were alone for the moment and just leaned in toward him, not saying a word. "You're not mad?"

"Yes, I'm mad, but not for why you might think. I'm mad that you had to do something like that in order to fit in, to cover. It pisses me off that everyone else can date and hold hands and make out in public, but we can't. It sucks that they get to do whatever they want, but if we so much as look at each other wrong they treat it like the end of the world."

Always the man of few words, Ben's response was simple. "Yeah."

We were quiet for a few minutes, just standing side by side, our bare arms touching periodically as we bumped against each other.

"Did you like it?" I asked him.

He thought for a minute before speaking. "Um, did it make my dick feel good? Yes. In my mind did it satisfy me and give me what I really wanted? No way."

"I've got to ask, but how did you get it up to… you know, do the deed?"

Ben blushed. It was so adorable.

"It wasn't easy. We'd been to see a movie earlier in the evening. Tom Cruise was in it, and he was looking hot for an old guy. When we got into bed at that motel that night, I turned the lights off and tried to pretend I was in bed with a naked, hot, hard Tom Cruise. I probably should send him a thank you note for that night, because he and I did wild stuff together, at least in my head. That was what got me hard and got me started. Can't say it was all that spectacular. I tried to make it last, which meant I had to stop a lot and kiss her while… you know, we were doing it. All the guys in the locker room talk about how hard it is to get a woman off, whatever that means, and how you have to do it long and slow. So I tried. She never did seem to have a big moment, not like guys get when we cum, you know. But I did what I could."

We were quiet for a few minutes as we stood there side by side. "Was it just that one time?" I asked suddenly.

Ben hesitated. Okay, so no. "Um, no. We did it a couple more times after that."

"You gave Tom Cruise quite a workout, didn't you?" I tried to joke to mask my anger.

"Are you mad?" Ben asked somewhat meekly.

"Yes. But like I told you, not at you. We didn't know each other then, did we?"

"No. You weren't here yet. It was last May right before school was getting out."

And that reminded me. "What the fuck was that about you quitting school?" His mom had told me this a long time back, but I hadn't talked with Ben about it, so I decided to try to convince him to go back.

Still looking down, Ben told me. "Yeah. I did. I didn't tell them or anything, but I told the people I knew that I wouldn't be back."

"Why not? You're going to be a senior. The end, graduation, is so close."

"School was a struggle for me. And then my dad died, and I had so much work to do here. It just seemed like school was a luxury I couldn't afford anymore."

"How did your mom take the news?" I asked him.

"She didn't like it, but there wasn't much she could do about it. If you're over sixteen, you can quit. I'm seventeen."

"But you're so close. A diploma will make a difference when you try to get jobs in the future."

"Look at me," Ben said angrily. "This is my job. This is my life. I'm a farmer. I like it. It's what I am. It's what I do. It's what I'll always do."

I wasn't about to back off. "A diploma will make a difference. What if someday you need to go to the bank and ask to borrow money to build something or buy something you want to make more money here? They're gonna look at you, not just the financial you, but the rest of you. 'Did you graduate from high school' is going to be one of their questions. My dad sometimes talks about that banking shit so I've heard him talking about what they look for before approving loans."

"Really?"

"Would I lie to you? To the man I love?" I asked him with a gentle nudge to his side, which earned me a smile. Ben had the sweetest, cutest smile. Of course, I thought he had a cute everything. I wanted to wrap my arms around him right then and there but couldn't because another customer drove up just then, so we had to get back to work and earn our keep.

When we had time to get back to our original conversation, I asked Ben an important question. "Um, I've been thinking."

"Okay. Should I be worried?"

"I'm not sure. But I think I should be."

"I'm confused. Start over, please."

"When that girl was here earlier...."

"Amelia?"

"Yeah, that girl," I said, trying to put as much sneer in my voice as possible.

"What about her?"

"She sounded quite, um, attached to you. She was talking about you two doing stuff together like you were a couple."

"Yep, I heard her."

"Is that true? Are you a couple?"

"Hell no," Ben instantly answered.

"Does she know that?"

Ben sighed, never a good way for him to answer a question. "I've been thinking about it too. I thought she'd have gotten the message—"

"Didn't you tell her directly?"

"Um, not quite."

"Ben!" I scolded him. "Why would you do something like that? So she thinks that you two are still together in some form?"

"We're not," he told me.

"You know that, but that's only half of the equation."

"I hate confrontations," Ben said. After that he was quiet, but I could tell that he was deep in thought.


THE REMAINDER of that month was a flurry of activity. Ben and I continued to work from sunup to sundown seven days a week. I was perpetually tired after a couple weeks at that pace, but so was he. The human body can only take so much before it tires out. I don't know how Ben did it day in and day out for years on end.

Never before had I looked forward to the arrival of the school year as much as I did that year. And remember that I didn't especially have a lot to look forward to that year. I'd lost all of my friends, all the people I'd grown up with and gone to school with for years in May. I'd never even had the chance to tell them good-bye or to tell them what was happening. And who knew what my former friend Mark was telling them in my absence. I could only imagine some of the rumors that would be flying around when school started again back in the city and people saw my sister there but not me. There was no question— there would be talking going on.

But I wasn't there. I was here, so I had to make the best of what I had. I'd never been in a situation like this before where I had to go into a brand-new group of people completely cold and try to fit in. The kids I'd be going to school with in a short while had all known one another for years—their whole lives probably. They'd have long ago sorted out the cliques and the in crowd and the out crowd—and then I'd appear on the scene not knowing any of the things they took for granted. Oh, this was going to be so much fun. Not!

Ben and I worked like big farm animals getting as much done as possible. The days when my dad went into the city were the days we looked forward to the most. Those days we finished our work as fast as possible before racing back to my house, showering, and throwing ourselves at one another.

Typically our first time those nights was quick. It was hot and muggy, so we'd get all hot and sticky again, but oh, was it worth it. After some time just being still together, lying on our backs beside each other, we'd go for round two. That time we'd be more leisurely, more relaxed, and more passionate. It was no less intense than the first time, but it was more stretched out, it covered more time and made orgasm, when it happened, even more intense.

Every time with Ben was special, but those nights when we could take our time, with him in me or me in him, were the best. He'd get aggressive for a few minutes and then slow down, stop even, and just lie long and swollen inside my body while we kissed. Ben was one hell of a kisser. His lips were made for kissing, and even more than that, his lips were made for kissing mine. When he kissed me, it was almost like he was trying to suck out my soul and join it with his. There was a particular intensity to his kisses that made me pant and want them to go on and on and on.

When Ben firmed up again, he'd go back at what he'd been doing. Sometimes, rarely, he'd stop again and we'd have another lull in our lovemaking, but usually that second time was the time he rang my bell, and I did the same for him.

We tried lots of variations, lots of different positions, but my favorite remained one of us on his back with the other on top of him. I loved that for one simple reason—I could look into Ben's eyes—those eyes that seemed to go on forever and encompass such an old soul. I loved looking into his eyes, especially while we were joined together.

We decided that there was something especially good for Ben on his back and me sitting down on his erection. I didn't think that was going to be all that great, but it was, because it seemed to push him in deeper than I expected, changing the angle a little bit, doing good things inside of me, and allowing me or Ben to jerk me off while he fucked me. In that position we could aim for getting off at roughly the same time, which was erotic as hell.

The bottom line for me was it didn't really matter what position we were in. As long as Ben was naked and in bed with me any position was good because the main need was already satisfied. I was in bed with the man I loved.

In late August, after we'd been working flat out for weeks on end, we were both freaking exhausted. We'd gone to my house after work to have our personal time together. Usually Ben got up, dressed, and left after we were finished. We both hated it, but that was the way it had to work. Only that one night we fell asleep—both of us naked and in my bed together.

When I woke up in the morning, I was in a dead panic, freaking out that we'd get caught or had already been caught. I jumped out of bed, stubbing my toe on the corner of a heavy dresser that sat in the wrong place, and dashed to the window. And, I thanked God my dad's car wasn't parked where it usually was when he was there. He must've still been in New York. I wanted to fall to my knees and give thanks.

I decided to be doubly sure, so I walked down the hall to his bedroom and looked in. His bed was made up and had not been slept in.

I listened at the top of the stairs, but the house was quiet. I could finally breathe a little easier.

As much as I hated to, I had to go wake Ben and get him up so we could get back to work. He, of course, went through exactly the same thing I had when I first woke up, but at least I was quickly able to calm him down and reassure him there was no problem.

# Chapter Sixteen
# School

THE FOLLOWING night was our regular dinner with my dad and Melinda at their house. I was really pleased when Ben, who was usually quiet as a church mouse during dinners, spoke up and told his mother he had made a decision and wanted to tell her about it.

"What's that, dear?" she asked, looking worried.

"I've given it a lot of thought, and I think I will go back to school when it starts next week."

"Ben! I'm so glad you decided to do that." She jumped up and hugged her son, which made him smile. It made me smile too. It also made me a little sad because I didn't have a parent I had any interest in hugging, although it was also good because I had a parent who clearly had no interest in hugging me.

So without talking about it, I lived vicariously through Melinda and Ben as they hugged in joy that evening. This was the first I was hearing about Ben's decision, so I guessed he'd been thinking about it for a while, maybe even thinking about me encouraging him to go for his last year and graduate.

When we sat down, Ben added one final thing that I also hadn't expected. "You know I wasn't a very good student, but now that we've got Einstein over here," he pointed his thumb vaguely in my direction, "I'm hoping I can get him to help me on some of the stuff."

Before I could answer, my father immediately said, "Absolutely. Adam's not a half-bad student, so he can help you." Way to go, Dad. Thanks for offering my services again without asking me. And then there was that whole "not half-bad" thing. Was that supposed to be a compliment? Words of encouragement? If so, he needed to work on it a bit.

The following morning Ben borrowed his mother's truck and drove us both to the school we'd be going to in a few days. They automatically assumed he'd be there, so this trip was for him to introduce me to the administration and let them know that I'd be a new student starting school there along with everyone else.

The place was a bit of a zoo. There was only one woman there who was working, and it seemed like the telephone never stopped ringing the entire time we were there. I didn't know if this was the way it always was, but she seemed to be beyond frazzled. In the few seconds when he had her attention, Ben asked if we were in the same classes. Ben laid it on thick, talking about how I didn't know anyone in the community except for him. He was just starting to talk about how hard it must be to start in a new school when the damned telephone started to ring again. I wanted to rip the thing off her desk and throw it out the window for her.

We waited for her to finish the latest phone call, but before she could say anything, the phone rang again. She shook her head in obvious frustration.

As she headed to the telephone, Ben asked, "Can I give Adam a quick tour of the building?"

"Of course, Ben."

"Thanks, Mrs. Smith," he told the woman behind the counter, flashing his biggest smile. Apparently I wasn't the only one who liked his smiles and nearly melted when they were turned their way.

While she took yet another phone call, Ben led me out of the office.

"Do you know her? It sounded like you do."

"Only since I've gone to this school. She's always done the same job."

As Ben walked me through the school, I realized several things, but first and foremost was that the school was significantly smaller than the schools I'd gone to in the city. There were only something like twenty-five classrooms in the entire building and that was for grades ten, eleven, and twelve. I didn't see how that was going to work, but Ben reminded me that we were in a rural, agricultural area where everything was spaced out and no one was close to anyone else because of the size of the farms. I guess he had a point, but still I'd have to see it to really understand it.

Since the place wasn't all that large, I didn't have to struggle to remember where everything was located.

"Here's where we'll have English with Mrs. Mann," he explained. "And then math with Mrs. Whitehead."

"How do you know who the teachers will be?" I asked him, confused.

"Simple. They're the only ones who teach those classes."

"You mean that there's only one person who teaches senior English?"

"Yes. She also teaches some of the lower levels as well, but she's the only one who teaches the senior class."

I shook my head. Unbelievable. "Where I went to school, there were a lot of teachers, and you never knew who you were gonna get until your first day."

"Wow. I'd hate that," he told me. "Since I've been around these folks for years, I know what they're like and what to expect."

"Must be nice," I muttered.

As we made our way back to the entrance, we had to pass the office. Mrs. Smith was on the telephone again—surprise, surprise. But as we passed by the office, she motioned us to come in. Holding the phone away from her head for a moment, she said, "Here's your schedules. I made your schedules the same except for two periods in the morning where I couldn't."

"Thanks, Mrs. Smith," he told her as she got back onto the telephone.

In the truck on the way back to the farm, I told Ben how great it was to have our class schedules and to know when we would and wouldn't be together.

As HARD as it was to believe, it was Labor Day weekend, a three-day weekend, not that it mattered much to me and the hours I worked, but it was a bookend that marked the beginning of something new. The Tuesday following the holiday, Ben and I were at the bus stop waiting for our ride to our first day of school. Since it was the first day, we were both traveling light. I knew that wouldn't last, but for now we only had a couple of notebooks. I might not have had much to carry, but I was weighed down with nervousness and anxiety.

I couldn't believe it, but when the bus came, it was nearly full. It was also loud—very loud. There were not two seats together, so Ben and I were forced to sit apart. He got a seat first and I had to go back farther into the bus, even though what I wanted to do was to crawl into Ben's lap.

My butt had barely hit the seat before someone was leaning over from behind me to ask, "Yo, new kid, who the fuck are you?"

"Um, hi, I'm Adam."

"You a farmer?"

"I guess."

"Where you from?"

"New York."

"You're in New York, dipshit."

"New York City."

"What the hell are you doing here?" she demanded as she smacked a wad of gum.

"Damned if I know," I told her, shaking my head. "You'd have to ask my dad." And then I had to stretch the truth a wee tiny bit. "He thinks farming is the life he wants."

"Is he nuts?" she asked.

"Probably."

The noise, and the interrogation, continued through the entire thirty-minute ride to school. By the time we got there, there was not a single empty seat on the entire bus. There were little kids, big kids, and just about every age in between. The bus went to three different schools, getting to our school first where about half the students got off.

I hadn't noticed before but wished I had—while I waited for those ahead of me to get off, I saw that the seat Ben had taken was beside the girl who'd come to the market during the summer—the one he'd dated and had sex with. Had I realized who was there, I would have taken the seat and sent him back to find another one. But by the time I realized who Ben was seated beside, they'd had half an hour to sit and talk. I obviously couldn't tell what they were talking about, but I could see they were talking. I was not happy, especially with the way she was clinging to him.

Since we hadn't been able to sit together, I expected Ben would be waiting beside the bus for me when I was finally able to make my way off the bus from where I'd been seated in the back. But he wasn't there when I got off the bus. I stood off to the side and looked all around but couldn't find Ben anywhere, which pissed me off. It didn't take a genius to figure out why, when I spotted the girl he'd been sitting beside dragging him away as quickly as possible. As the crowd of my new peers allowed me, I moved toward them as they moved away from me. I was finally able to catch up to them, but it took me a lot of work to make that happen. I stepped in front of them and addressed Ben. "You didn't wait for me."

But before Ben could answer, Amelia asked Ben, "Who's this?" From the frown on her face, it was clear I was not someone she wanted to deal with right then.

"Amelia, this is Adam. Adam, this is Amelia."

She held out a hand and loosely shook mine. "Hey," she told me with a definite lack of enthusiasm or sincerity. "So you're the new guy everyone's talking about?"

"Me?" I asked. Who was this "everybody" and why were they talking about me? If we'd been alone I could have asked Ben. I silently cursed Amelia and her presence that day and in general.

"Yeah, aren't you the one with the crazy father?"

"Excuse me?" I asked her.

But rather than answer my question, she took off, dragging Ben away from me again at close to breakneck speed. It took me a couple of seconds to believe that she'd really done what had just happened before

I could react. I moved with the crowd in the hallways. The ebb and flow of people kept me from regaining ground on them. I kept them in sight, but wasn't able to close the distance between us.

I was mad—at her for taking him away, at Ben for letting her take him away. The way she clung to Ben, never leaving his side, never letting go of his arm, I could tell immediately that she was going to be trouble. She clearly had her eyes, at least, on Ben and wanted him. I didn't need the competition. I didn't want the competition. I trusted Ben, but it pissed me off that she could do that and I couldn't. It also pissed me off that just when I needed him, he was busy with her hanging all over him.

I took a deep breath trying to calm myself down. My split second analysis was simple: Ben might not have thought he was still dating Amelia, but that wasn't the way she saw it. In her eyes, it appeared that they were still very much a couple, and she wanted Ben all to herself. It wasn't that she was against me necessarily, but she didn't want anyone or anything to distract Ben from her.

As they walked away, I watched how she clung to Ben like he was a life preserver and she was drowning in a sea of rough water. She was also talking nearly nonstop, and it looked like Ben was being polite and listening to her. Only once did he glance back toward me, but I'm not sure he saw me.

We all were in the same homeroom, so at least we shared a common destination. By the time I got into the room, though, Amelia had dragged Ben to the far side of the room and put him in a seat by the wall with herself in the seat right beside him. I was determined to get over near him and at least be close to Ben. He'd promised me that we'd sit together and while he didn't appear interested in keeping his word, I wasn't going to let him off the hook quite so easily.

I was headed their way to grab a seat at least near Ben when I got waylaid by someone. Just when I wanted to get over to Ben, there was suddenly another person in front of me, blocking my movement.

"Hi, you're new, aren't you?" It was a girl I obviously didn't know. She seemed entirely too perky for words.

"Um, yes."

"Hi, I'm Brandi, with an *i*."

"Hi, Brandi. I'm Adam… with an *a*."

"Hi, Adam. You new to the area?"

"Just moved here in May. I guess that means I'm not so new anymore."

I glanced Ben's way. By that point I was close enough to hear anything he said. What I heard was him say, "I promised Adam I'd sit with him because he's new and doesn't know anybody."

For a fleeting moment I had some hope, but that was squashed quickly when I heard her tell him, "Look, he's talking with Brandi. See, he's already making friends and knows somebody besides you."

Ben didn't say anything, for which I silently cursed him. I tuned in to Brandi as she said, "I've lived here my whole life. Can't wait to get away. It must suck to have to move here."

"It's different," I told her.

Further conversation was not possible because the teacher was trying to get everyone into seats to get started with something—attendance, I think. Of course when I turned around and headed to where I wanted to be, there were no empty seats anywhere near Ben. This day was not working out the way I had anticipated. I paused long enough to look toward him while I tried to figure out what to do. Amelia kept talking to him a mile a minute, so he was focused entirely on her.

Ben glanced quickly at me as I passed, looking unhappy and maybe a bit meek, which I found to be an odd expression on someone as big and tall and muscular as he was. It also told me that we had some things to talk about that night.

Homeroom was nothing special. It was just a place where we were counted as present or not each day. The only thing that sucked was that the homeroom teacher told us the seats we were in were our permanent seats for the entire year and that we were to go to them every day. He added that there would be no switching. I was screwed. Ben was halfway across the room with that woman, and I was stuck in the back with the delinquents. Sighing, I was silently cursing my father yet again for ruining my life.

Homeroom lasted twenty minutes, which felt like forever. Everyone around me had someone to talk with. The delinquents had one another. But the only person I knew and wanted to talk with wasn't anywhere near me. I was pissed. He didn't even look back my way, which only pissed me off even more.

Our first class was English. I don't know how it happened, but I spotted Ben without Amelia Velcroed to his side. He took a seat in the middle of the room, and I was actually able to get close enough to be able to grab the seat beside him. I was just about to feel good for the first time that day when Amelia reappeared and slid into the seat on the other side of Ben. Ignoring me completely, she instantly started talking to Ben once again.

While we waited for everyone to arrive and get settled, of course there was a lot of talking. It sounded like everyone knew one another, which I guess made sense since they'd all grown up together and gone to the same school their entire lives. So I sat alone in the crowded room and mentally cursed the universe for kicking me that morning.

Moving from one school to another was difficult on so many levels, not just because you had to leave behind everyone and everything you knew and start all over again. It was also tough because your new school assumed you had the basics they had taught in the earlier grades. But if you went to a different school in another place, you might not have covered exactly the things they wanted or expected.

There were some clear differences between my earlier grades and what these folks had done, as quickly became apparent, but fortunately they seemed to be in my favor. It turned out that one of the books we were going to read that semester was one I'd read the previous year in my English class back in the city. That was fine. I'd read it again. As I recalled it wasn't too bad. The rest of the stuff looked new to me, but not scary at all.

I took some notes and doodled a little in my notebook while the teacher talked. Her style was good, walking around, talking with us, kind of like making teaching into a conversation. I liked it, and it also gave me a chance to hear a few of my classmates speak. I learned a lot about them by listening to how they spoke and what they had to say. I'm a pretty good judge of character, I think, so as I watched and listened I could see which ones were going to amount to something, which ones were total losers, and which ones were going to potentially be troublemakers. Not that I expected them to automatically do something nasty, but I thought they had the capacity to do something unsavory.

Ben and I were separated for the next two periods, the only time we'd be apart. I hated seeing him go another way from where I was supposed to go. I especially hated having a Study Hall period when I didn't have anything with me to read or a puzzle to do or something. If I was home I'd have a book of Sudoku puzzles with me in my backpack, but those were all back in the city—where I wasn't.

It turned out that the teacher in charge of the Study Hall realized that with the first day just beginning, no one would have homework or anything they needed to study, so she let everyone basically mix and mingle, talk with friends, so long as it didn't get too out of hand. I could see how people automatically sorted themselves out into what were most likely long-standing friendships or cliques. I didn't know which one I fit in, nor did I really care much.

Of course I didn't know anyone, so no one automatically came over to talk with me. I hated how obvious it was that I was the only one sitting in his chair. I had found an old magazine lying in the back of the room, which I'd grabbed. Even though it was quite out of date, at least it gave me something to read to try to pass the fifty minutes I had to spend in the room. Near the end of the period as people were returning to their seats to reclaim their bags and get ready for the bell to sound, one girl did smile and say hi to me and ask me my name. I gave it to her, but the bell rang before I could return the favor and ask her name. It would give me something to do the next day.

The next period I was again apart from Ben. I now was taking the class he had taken the period before while he took the Study Hall I'd just taken. The class size was about half what the first class had been. Instead of desks and chairs in a row, all of them were arranged in a complete circle so everyone could see everyone else. I hated it when teachers wanted the interactive experience. As quiet as he was, I'm sure Ben hadn't been very fond of it either.

At lunchtime I started looking for Ben, since we'd planned to have lunch together. I looked in all the likely places where I thought he might be—his locker, outside the classroom he'd just left, the men's room—but I couldn't find him anywhere. We only had a limited amount of time for lunch, and since the halls were clearing I had to head off to lunch or potentially have someone ask me why I wasn't where I was supposed to be. I was hungry and I didn't want to talk to anyone about where I was supposed to be so I headed to the cafeteria.

Since my dad couldn't cook to save his life, and I didn't have time to do much because I was working on the Taylor farm constantly, I hadn't tried to bring anything. My dad had given me money to buy lunch, which was good because what they had actually looked and smelled great. They had choices and they looked a lot better than the industrial food I'd had at school before.

Choices made, money paid, it was time for the tough part. I'd been dreading this part from the first time I'd seen the cafeteria. The room could seat several hundred people at the same time and as I feared, there was someone at every table. It was also incredibly loud. The sound of two hundred adolescents all talking at the same time, some of them very animated and energized, combined to make something approximating a dull roar. I'd always hated lunch because of the noise. I liked to read at lunch, but the noise was so bad that I'd always found it distracting.

But noise or not, I needed to find someplace to eat, so I started looking around the room for an empty place where I could slip in and not be in the way or too noticeable. I spotted a place and headed that way. On the way to my destination, though, I spotted something that almost made me lose my appetite—Ben, once again with Amelia firmly attached to his side. She actually was sitting with one of her arms looped through one of his arms. They were at a table that was absolutely filled with people, a mix of guys and girls. There were so many people that a couple of them had to stand behind others who were seated. A couple of the guys looked like athletic types. They were all laughing and joking together about something. I couldn't tell what, nor did I care.

I was pissed. I was really pissed. I know I was probably being unfair, but he'd told me before we started school that we'd have lunch together every day. He'd promised me that he wouldn't just leave me alone in a place where I didn't know anyone. I hadn't asked him—he'd offered it all on his own. And stupid me, I'd believed him. I had been counting on my time together with Ben and was pissed that he'd unilaterally changed the plans that we'd made before school started. As I passed by his table, I deliberately slowed down a bit and looked his way. He did look up and spotted me, giving me a weak smile that could be taken any number of ways. Scowling at him with what I hoped was unmistakable disappointment, somewhat angrily I took my spot at another table and ate my lunch, no longer really caring what it was or how it tasted. No one sat beside me, although there were others at the table, but that was fine by me.

The minute I was finished, I headed to the school library, which was provided as a quiet alternative to the noisy cafeteria. On the way, I deliberately walked by Ben's table and gestured with my head for him to join me. It looked like he tried to stand, but Amelia held tight to him and pulled him back down. She said something to him, but I couldn't hear it. Whatever it was, it was clear that he wasn't going to come join me even for a few minutes. I'd like to know where my ballsy Ben had gone and where this new one had come from. I wanted my Ben back, not this meek imitation Ben.

I spotted other students outside in front of the school. It was a beautiful day, so I changed directions and went out. The sun felt wonderful, warming my face. A bench in the sun was calling to me, so I had to answer it. I dropped my head back a little and let the sun work its magic, warming my face and driving away some of my anger. It tried real hard but it did not fully succeed.

What the hell had happened? I just wanted to know why Ben had changed so many of the plans we had. It was tough enough being apart from him for two periods, but now it had been the entire first half of the day, which plain sucked. We'd spent months and months together, working all summer long seven days a week in recent weeks from sunup to sundown. Ben had been my constant companion in all of that, so it felt weird to now be alone.

Had all of that been a lie? Had he been deceiving me? I didn't understand. Ben was a big, strong guy. Why was he letting Amelia boss him around? I didn't understand.

It felt like a part of me was missing, like I'd laid something down and walked away and forgotten it. I decided to blame my dad for this whole thing, because it was his fault that I wasn't back home with my friends. But then I did what I did every time I thought such thoughts—I remembered that if we hadn't come out to the country, I never would have gotten to meet Ben, and to fall in love with Ben. And despite my anger at the moment, I did love him.

My break outdoors in the sun had felt so freaking good that I hated it when I heard the bell sound, telling me to get to my next class. Acting something like an old man, I dragged myself up off the bench and sort of half shuffled back toward the door and into the school to rejoin the moving sea of people, all headed somewhere at the same time. I had to check my cheat sheet in my pocket to remember where I was supposed to be next. I could find my way around the building with no problem. The problem I had was that I couldn't remember which room I was supposed to be in next.

Of course it was at the far end of the building and time was getting short, so I had to hustle. And as always seems to happen, the faster you need to go, the slower everyone around you seems to be. I barely made it through the door before the bell sounded again. The teacher was standing by the door and the instant the bell sounded he closed the door. I could see he was one of those who had issues about time. Good to know.

This was our science class, so the room was set up with a series of raised lab benches with stools for two people to sit at each bench. Ben had especially focused on this class before school started. I remembered him telling me just a couple of days earlier that science and math were two classes that had given him trouble the previous year, and how very much he was looking forward to having me with him in those classes. I had assured him that I'd had no problems in either class before, and in fact, was quite fond of my math classes.

But any thoughts I'd had in the back of my mind about sitting with Ben were squashed when I walked in and saw him sitting at the very first lab bench with—who else?—Amelia. As I walked slowly past them, Ben didn't even have the balls to look up at me that time. When I spotted her arm still wrapped through his, I wanted to rip it away and yell, "Mine!" I didn't say that, but I did mutter something that only Ben could hear. "Thanks, Ben. Nice of you to hold a seat for me again." I know he heard me, because I saw him jerk as if he'd been given an electric jolt. I made my way to the back of the room once again to the only open seat.

I didn't get to pick my lab partner. Circumstances picked my lab partner. How to describe him? Nerd? Geek? Bumpkin? Hick? Take your pick. They all worked. In other words, he was everything I wasn't. He was also the one who no one else had wanted to sit with, which was quite telling in such a closed group where everyone had been together all their lives.

I wanted to be polite, so I looked at him and whispered, "Adam" as I extended my hand in greeting. He looked at my hand as if it was something novel, hesitating for a moment before he did likewise.

"Bill" was all he said, his voice sounding more refined and much deeper than I had anticipated based on his appearance. While the teacher got himself organized and talked about rules and crap like that, I carefully took a better look at my lab partner. He wasn't so awkward-looking on second glance. It was his clothes that looked awkward and out of place. When I looked beyond his clothes at the outline of the body beneath them, I saw that he was actually fairly solid-looking. He wasn't muscular like Ben, but he was no ninety-eight pound weakling either.

Some residual acne and a pair of the world's most hideous glasses were the main other things that caught my attention first. Without being too obvious, I tried to look at his face and imagine him without the glasses and without the acne. I had to look away when he caught me looking at one point. He didn't say anything, but he looked at me suspiciously after that, so I had to stop.

As I had feared, where we sat was to be our permanent seat for the entire semester, so any hopes I might have had about sitting with and working with Ben went out the window officially with that announcement. I slouched on my stool the best one can slouch on a stool and tried to endure the fifty-minutes. Before I left, Bill spoke to me, surprising me with his directness. "Sorry you got stuck with me. I know everybody tries to steer clear of me."

"Right back atcha," I told him. "You get stuck with the new guy who nobody knows or trusts."

I was surprised when he actually snickered a bit at that.

"We'll be a good pair," he said before we walked out together. I followed behind him and noticed that if one got rid of the clothes, he had what looked like a really great body. Then I remembered Ben and his awesome everything, and I mentally slapped myself for looking at another guy. Of course then I instantly remembered how abandoned I had been for most of the day by Ben and his awesomeness, and I took another look at Bill's backside. It seemed only fair to me.

The rest of the day was pretty much the same. Amelia got Ben beside her nearly every time and somehow managed to sidetrack me so I wasn't even close to him. I only once got to sit next to Ben for the remainder of the afternoon. He had been free of her for a moment before our final class of the day. I don't know where she was or how he'd gotten free, but he had done it somehow, so I took the seat immediately beside him. I hadn't even had a chance to turn toward him and say "hi" before Amelia was in front of me glaring down at me.

"That's my seat," she said to me very sharply.

What the fuck was I supposed to say to that? I tried to be polite. "Um, sorry, I'm here."

"Move," she told me angrily. In case I hadn't heard her tone of voice, the look on her face was crystal clear.

I looked to Ben who was trying his best to ignore the whole thing.

"I got here first," I tried to explain to her.

"I don't care. Move," she ordered.

While Amelia had been fussing at me, the bell had sounded and the teacher was clearly ready to start the class. Since we were at the very front of the room, though, it was obvious that there was an issue front and center in the classroom.

"Is there a problem here?" I heard the teacher ask.

"He's in my seat," Amelia told her.

"Young man?" I guess that was directed at me.

"I got here first. The seat was empty. It's beside somebody I know. I took it. I like it."

"Amelia, take another seat so we can begin."

Amelia stared daggers at me and informed me, "This isn't over." She then "accidentally" spilled a thirty-six-ounce cup of Coke she was holding all over me as she moved past me.

"What the fuck are you doing?" I yelled at her as she soaked me completely.

"Oh, I'm so sorry," she apologized with such fakeness that everyone had to see it.

I jumped up out of the seat, trying to shake some of the liquid off me. But there was just too much of it. It covered me and had soaked into my shirt, which was now sticking to me everywhere. Thirty-six ounces was a lot of liquid. I sneered at her as I started toward the door.

"Where are you going?" the teacher asked.

"She just poured a whole bucket of Coke all over me. I'm soaked. I'm going to try to dry off." I was pissed, at Amelia, at Ben, at the day, and now at the teacher. Perhaps there was a harshness to my tone. It wouldn't surprise me if there were. She looked unhappy with me, which was definitely not the way I liked to start a new teacher-student relationship.

"Use the sink over there," she told me, pointing toward a sink I hadn't spotted before that was at the back of the room. I'd been surprised to see a sink in an earlier classroom, but I'd noticed one in several rooms by that point, so I guessed they were part of the school's design. "And please be quick about it. We have a lot to cover today."

I stopped dead in my tracks. Surely she wasn't serious. It was impossible to miss how soaked I was. Slowly I turned to face the teacher directly, my anger growing in intensity with each degree of my turn. I felt my shoulders hunch forward like a prizefighter getting ready to go into the ring. My face muscles stiffened. I also felt the fingers of each hand form into fists.

"Excuse me?" I asked quietly. Where that calm came from I had no idea.

"Please be quick about it. We have a lot of material to cover today."

"I'm soaked," I told her again, since she'd seemed to miss that important fact.

"There are paper towels by the sink," she added, as if that would solve everything.

I made my way to the sink, dripping every step of the way. The paper towels just weren't cutting it, so I did the only thing I could—I unbuttoned my new shirt and peeled it off my shoulders. I wasn't uncomfortable being seen without my shirt on, like I would have been at one time. After an entire summer of working on the farm with Ben, I'd built some good muscles, and I knew that everything was in the right place and looked pretty damned good, if I did say so myself. And after working in the sun all summer, I also had a nice tan on top of the muscles. I heard a couple of the girls nearby whisper something to one another, but I couldn't make out what they were saying.

"What on earth are you doing?" the teacher demanded. I could hear the edge in her voice. When I realized that she was addressing me, I held up the still dripping shirt as if that would explain everything.

I was uncomfortable, not because I was bare-chested, but because I was the focus of everyone's attention. I was going to be absolutely miserable sitting in wet clothes for the last period of the day, especially sticky wet clothes. I just hoped that the Coke didn't stain my new shirt.

"Please take your seat."

If that was the way she was going to play it, I'd go along. Bare-chested, I turned and started back to where it had all gone so terribly wrong. And of course, wouldn't you know it, but someone else had already taken my seat. I'd had all I could take from her, so I just stood in front of her and stared.

"I told you to take your seat," the teacher repeated with clear impatience.

"There's someone in my seat," I told her calmly, reporting the obvious.

"Take another seat."

"This *is* my seat." I was wet, my new shirt was potentially ruined, and I'd been fighting an unanticipated battle all day long. This was war.

"Take an open seat."

"This. Is. My. Seat," I repeated slowly as I stared at Amelia. The flags were down, and we had a catfight going. "You saw me sitting in this seat. Do you deny seeing me sitting here? This is my seat."

"Take another seat, please."

I didn't move but merely crossed my arms over my bare chest and stood my ground. A quick glance at Ben showed me that I wasn't going to get any support out of him. I don't know where my Ben had disappeared to, but he was gone, replaced by this new guy I didn't especially like. No, that's too weak. I hated this new Ben. All summer long I'd seen an entirely different Ben—an aggressive, forceful, decisive Ben. I didn't know who this guy was in his place.

When I didn't move for a full minute, and of course neither did Amelia, I think the entire class held its collective breath to see what was going to happen next. The teacher grabbed something on her desk, checked off something on a piece of paper and handed it to me. "Report to the principal's office immediately."

She held her piece of paper out to me, but I didn't move. I glanced down at the piece of paper in her hand, but I didn't make any move to take it from her.

"So you're not going to teach anything today after all?" I asked her.

"I most certainly am, once I finish with you wasting our valuable time. We have a lot of material to cover today."

"You had better not cover anything today without me here, or you'll be getting a visit from my father. You don't know him, but trust me—once someone goes up against him, they never forget him. When he goes up against an opponent in court, he takes no prisoners in order to win. He will not be happy that his son was kept from learning today and unfairly disadvantaged on his first day in your school and in your class in particular."

We were all so far in now that there was no way anyone was going to come out a winner in this mess. The only question was who was going to blink first. It turned out the teacher had more spine than I had anticipated. "Take this and get out of my classroom now," she ordered.

I smiled sweetly at her.

I left Ben and the class of people who were all transfixed by what they'd just watched and made my way to the main office, still shirtless. I wanted to stop in the men's room and wash some or all of my body first, but I decided it was more effective to go as I was. Needless to say, I got attention walking in shirtless. The same woman who had helped Ben get me assigned to the same classes—fat lot of good that had done—immediately came forward, "Yes?"

I handed her the note. I wasn't sure what it said or meant since I hadn't taken the time to read it.

"Who gave this to you?"

"I have no idea what her name is. I twice tried to introduce myself and be friendly, and she never reciprocated." I was calling on all the big words I knew, all the things I'd heard my father say over the years. I might not have listened to every word he said, but after hearing the same things over and over and over again, some of it had started to sink in and stick with me.

"Why are you not wearing a shirt?" she asked.

"Another student poured a huge Coke drink over me."

She immediately stepped away, knocked on an open door close at hand, and waited as a perfectly average middle-aged man stepped out.

"Hello, I'm Principal Robinson, and I understand that we have a problem. Come into my office and we'll talk."

Once seated in his office, I politely waited for him to get settled.

"I don't recognize you," he started.

"I'm Adam, Adam Caldwell. I'm new. Today's my first day. Can't say my first day has been all that good, what with another student assaulting me and all." I had no idea if what she'd done was assault, but it couldn't hurt to say it.

"Tell me what happened," he asked, so I did. I recounted the entire tale, making sure I was entirely accurate and perfectly factual. He nodded in acknowledgement after he had paid careful attention to me throughout the entire recitation of my story. "Students are not allowed to have beverages in class," he told me, as if that solved everything.

I held up my wet shirt and said, "Well, I have proof that either she broke the rule or it rained in that classroom this afternoon."

"Wait one moment," he told me while he stepped out briefly. A few minutes later he was back. "We don't seem to have a file for you, which means that we don't have any of your transfer records from your old school. We are therefore not legally able to enroll you or have you here."

Oh, this was not good—it was so not good. This was all my dad's doing, so it was going to be up to him to sort it out. "I'll call my dad." But I wasn't going to be put off. "But tell me what we do about this Amelia person and her assault?" To make my point I held up my very wet shirt for him to take, feel, examine, do whatever he wanted to do. Of course he did not make any move to take or touch my shirt since it looked disgusting.

"One thing at a time," he said, holding up one of his hands.

"Fine. You should know that I don't forget, and as soon as this is all worked out, and I'm technically part of your school, I will be right back in here to take up this issue where you are making me leave it today." He didn't blink. "And since I can't do anything through proper channels here, when I leave here, I'll call the police and report it to them. You won't touch it, but I'm sure they won't be quite as dismissive.

"There's a couple of things you should know about me," I explained to him. "If I'm wrong, I'll admit it. If I've made a mistake, I own up to it. But if I'm right about something, I don't back down. I stand up for myself."

My dad had bought a cell phone for me to take to school so I'd have some way to reach him in the event of an emergency. Though who could have guessed that I would need it so soon. Still sitting in the principal's office chair, I called him, and he actually answered.

"Dad, I need you at the school. We've got a number of problems."

"What have you done?"

"I can't do anything since they don't know about me. You didn't have my current school records transferred. They've told me I have to leave."

He protested loudly enough that the principal could hear the words sitting a few feet away. I swear that I saw the man jump a little at the bark of my dad's voice. Welcome to my world. "They were supposed to be there long before this. I set that up nearly two months ago."

"Well, they don't have them," I told him, "so they don't want me. I need you to come get me."

"Fine," he muttered. "I'm on my way."

"And then there's the matter of the assault," I added before he could hang up. I knew that would catch his interest.

"What assault?" he yelled.

"The assault on me in my last class. You're going to have a field day with this one. I look forward to seeing the cutthroat approach you're known for. Should I call the police now, or do you want to do that when you get here?"

"I'm on my way," he told me.

I disconnected the call and sat back to wait.

"What does your father do for a living?" the principal asked.

"He's a lawyer, a defense attorney."

"And where are you from?"

"The City. New York City."

"Was your move quite recent?"

"No. We got here in May. We've been here all summer."

"Where are you living? I assume you're renting some place."

"No. My dad owns a huge farm back up in the hills." I vaguely gestured with my hand. "Melinda Taylor uses some of it."

"The old Caldwell farm?"

"Yeah, I guess."

"That place has been empty for years."

"My dad's grandfather left it to him. He got a sudden hankering to play farmer, so here we are."

"Isn't he still a lawyer?"

"Yes, he is. He does a lot of work remotely, and he drives back to the city once a week for meetings and stuff."

"Why don't you go to the men's room and clean yourself up a bit," he suggested.

"I can't," I told him definitively. "Chain of evidence and all that, you know. The crime scene investigators get pissed if you do anything to disrupt their evidence. They won't be happy that the evidence in the classroom has been disrupted, so I need to preserve what's left."

"I don't think that will be an issue," he told me with a smile.

I looked at him and raised an eyebrow, inviting an explanation of that last statement.

"I will have a talk with Miss Johnson."

"A talk." It wasn't a question, but rather just a repetition of his words.

"Yes, that's what I said. I will have a talk with her about her behavior."

"That's it? A talk. No expulsion? No suspension? No arrest? I would think that her behavior would at least merit a suspension. An assault of one person on another is a very serious matter."

Unfortunately other matters required the principal's attention at that point, involving two students having a loud altercation just outside his door, so I had to sit out in the open area of the office and wait for my father to get there. Since my shirt was still wet I laid it down beside me. There was no way I was putting a wet shirt back on. I still didn't have a book to read or a puzzle to do, so I closed my eyes and stretched out the best I could in the present circumstance. I was wet, I was cold, and my skin was disgustingly sticky. I was so ready for this day to be over.

I heard the final bell ring, marking the end of my first day of school, and I had to say it had not gone at all as I had anticipated. I watched and heard students approach our location on their way to the buses to go home. That exodus was just beginning when my dad arrived. Never a man for pleasantries, he loudly demanded of the room, "Where is he?"

I pointed toward the principal's office, and he immediately marched over, knocked on the closed door, and opened it before his knock was even acknowledged. "We need to talk," he announced loudly to the principal. Without waiting for another word or invitation, he simply proceeded. "I was sorry to hear that your office has made such a grievous mistake that prevented my son from being enrolled."

"What do you mean, my office made a mistake?"

"I called my son's school in New York City. They sent his records to you as I had requested. I had asked that they be sent by some means that allowed tracking. They told me that a Ms. Cassidy signed for the package that was delivered here on August 14th. Now what you or your staff did with that package I cannot say, but that package contained the sum total of my son's school records, so I suggest you start tearing this place apart until you find it."

It was nice for once to see my father's wrath aimed at someone else. "Sir, Mr. Caldwell, I presume. Ms. Cassidy left employment here in mid-August, and she has not been replaced yet."

I saw my dad quickly glance around the room with its four desks, only three occupied. The fourth desk sat unused, looking more like a dumping ground for unwanted things than anything else. "Let's search her desk," my father announced. "I'm assuming it's this one." Without waiting for an invitation he stalked over and started rifling through the piles, looking for the recognizable FedEx packaging. There was only one such package, which he yanked out and threw toward the principal. "You, sir, need to get your house in order. I have paid tens of thousands of dollars in taxes for this school over the years, and I've never asked for anything for that money." He was on a roll. There was no stopping him now. "Now, when I ask you to educate my son for *one year*, this is the quality of service I get? I don't think so. Who is the superintendent and where can I find them? And give me a list of the school board members."

"Please," the principal said pleasantly. "Come into my office and we'll talk."

"Adam where's your shirt?" he asked, seeming to have just noticed that I was standing there shirtless. I walked over, picked it up, and handed it to him.

"Chain of evidence," I explained. "One Amelia Johnson poured an entire thirty-six ounce Coke over me—deliberately and maliciously. And he won't do anything about it." I gestured toward the principal. While that exchange was happening, I happened to look up and spotted Ben walking slowly past the glass wall of the office, obviously headed to the bus to go home. I should be with him. Hell, I should have been with him all day. "And there she is," I told them loudly, pointing to the girl still hanging on Ben's arm. Finally, something worked out time-wise in my favor that day. About fucking time!

"Get her in here," my dad ordered. When the principal didn't move, my dad stalked to the door and bellowed, "You, get in here now. Ben, did you witness the assault?" Most people hadn't seen my dad in action like I had over the years. When he was determined about something, he didn't pussyfoot around but made his desires crystal clear—and loud.

"Um," he started. "We were... we were in the same class."

Ben and Amelia came into the main office waiting area, both very hesitantly. "Our bus," Amelia said to Ben.

"You're missing it," my dad announced. "You sit," he ordered. He and the principal and Ben disappeared behind closed doors, and I could hear voices but couldn't make out what they were saying. Needless to say, I was not the only person who was trying to listen. Everyone in the office had been paying attention to the drama as it unfolded.

Amelia stood in the office, alternating between glaring at me and looking worried. Addressing the woman behind the counter, she announced, "I can't miss my bus. I don't have any way home if I don't take that bus." Without waiting for a response, she simply bolted and was gone.

A few minutes later when the office door opened, Ben quickly exited first. My dad looked out and didn't see Amelia. "Where the hell did she go?" he demanded.

"She left," I told him when no one else spoke up. He slammed the office door closed, and I heard his voice raised but still couldn't make out the words. Ben stood in the middle of the room looking lost. I certainly wasn't going to help him out, not until I had at least some explanation of what had happened that day, and even then I wasn't sure. Until I had that explanation, I wasn't feeling very hospitable toward him. In fact, I utterly ignored him, not even looking at him. He wisely didn't try to start a conversation. I returned to my chair, closed my eyes once again, and stretched out the best I could.

A few minutes later, my dad emerged from the office and announced, "Let's go home." The principal was right on his heels, immediately saying, "Mr. Caldwell." It took me a minute to realize he was talking to me. "Please accept my apologies for the mess you've had to go through on your first day here. We will all do our best to try to make the rest of your time here a much better experience."

"Thank you," I politely told him. "What do I do about the class that I missed this afternoon? Before she kicked me out, that woman told me she intended to teach, so if there was anything she covered that I'm expected to know for a test or whatever, what am I supposed to do? Am I just screwed right from the start? Am I at even more of a disadvantage right out of the gate?" I calmly asked him.

"We got homework already," Ben said, uttering the first words he'd said in my presence since leaving the principal's office.

"Don't worry about it. I'll talk with the teacher and make arrangements for you to get caught up with everyone else in the class. It's the least we can do."

Whatever my dad had said clearly had the guy scared and super accommodating. My dad seemed satisfied, so I followed him as he headed to the door.

When Ben didn't move, my dad ordered, "Come on, Ben."

The buses were long gone by that point, so it was wide open as we walked across the parking lot to my dad's car. Ben had always ridden in the front seat whenever we'd had to go anywhere in that car, simply because his legs were longer than mine and fit better in the front seat than in the backseat. But I wasn't in a sharing mood that afternoon. When he went to the front door, I stopped him by forcefully using Amelia's words, "That's my seat."

Ben didn't say a word but immediately went to the backseat. He didn't say a single word during the entire drive home that afternoon. We dropped him off at the front door to his house. As he was getting out, he told my dad, "Thanks for the ride." He offered nothing to me, and I certainly wasn't going to go out of my way to take the first step.

# Chapter Seventeen
# Round Two

BEN DIDN'T call or come near me that night, which was probably a reasonable thing. At the time, though, I was pissed and wanted him to come around and grovel. I really, really wanted him to grovel.

I didn't see Ben until the next morning. I was already at the bus stop as he walked slowly toward me and arrived minutes before the bus was due.

"Morning," he meekly said to me.

"Whatever," I muttered back at him.

I think he was waiting for me to say something, but I wasn't going to make it any easier for him, so I stood there looking out toward where the bus would be coming very soon.

"I'm sorry," he finally said softly.

"You should be," I told him. "What the hell happened yesterday?" I asked.

"I don't know. I should have said something, done something. I'm so sorry I didn't. She is so determined once she gets some idea in her head. She's hard to fight. I was so surprised by what she did that I didn't know how to handle it."

"Fine. But now we're stuck with a mess for the entire fucking school year. Nothing worked out like you'd told me it would. And we're stuck with it for the next nine months. You're not my lab partner in science like you'd wanted. We don't sit even close to each other in most of our classes. Everyone in our last class probably thinks I'm a monster. And on top of that, that woman is going to be next to you all day every single day. And that means not just sitting next to her in lectures, but working with her in science labs. You're going to have to talk with her and work together on projects. And I'm just left hanging in the wind, not knowing anybody.

"I got totally screwed yesterday, Ben. Nothing worked out the way you told me it would. You didn't even sit with me at lunch. You wouldn't even get up and go outside with me for a few minutes so we could talk. What was it, Ben? Were you embarrassed by me? Was that it? Because if that's the case, I'd like to know now so I don't waste any more of my time on you." I was getting really wound up, more than I had imagined or planned.

"Adam, no," Ben protested vigorously.

"Hell of a first day, don't you think? What am I supposed to do now, huh?"

"I know. I'm so sorry," he apologized again.

"Fine. But 'sorry' doesn't fix this mess."

"I'm so sorry," he apologized again.

"Okay. Fine. Just help me sort it out. What are we going to do to try to save at least something of what we'd planned? Or is it all over and gone before it even started?"

"Please, Adam. I'm so sorry. We'll still do what we planned."

"How, Ben?" I asked. "I certainly don't see any way for that to happen now."

The bus came, so he got a reprieve from having to answer my question. That morning there were actually two seats just across the aisle from one another. Ben took one, looking like he assumed I was automatically going to sit down in the other. I didn't. Instead, I kept walking back and took the empty seat beside Bill, my science lab partner. At least he'd been friendly to me. "Morning, Bill," I greeted him by name. He seemed surprised that I was talking with him. We ended up talking the entire time it took us to reach the school.

We kept talking as we walked together into the school, going right past Ben. Maybe I was being too harsh, but I'd been really badly burned yesterday, and I wasn't going to get over it that quickly. Ben had shown me that I couldn't count on him, which meant I had to create my own support network, and I had to start somewhere.

My second day was significantly better than my first day had been. Amelia wasn't there, for one. I could only assume she had been suspended or something. I didn't really care at the moment. I was just delighted to have her out of my way for now. It was so much nicer without her. Also, I had a new friend, Bill. As a senior, I was one of a relatively small group of students. It was a limited geographical area, and there weren't all that many of us, so we all saw one another fairly frequently throughout the day. I made a point of hanging out with him and always seeking him out if I had the chance. Unlike Ben, Bill never turned me away or snubbed me.

That day Ben and I were silently polite but also cautiously distant. We sat at the same table at lunch but didn't say much, since it wasn't the place to have any kind of a major conversation. I'd invited Bill to sit with me, so he and I talked. Ben was welcome to join in the conversation if he wanted, but he didn't.

During each of our classes, even though the seat beside Ben was open, I had to walk past it and take my seat in the back of the room, which only helped to reignite my anger from the first day. Other than acknowledging each other's presence as I passed him, conversation was nonexistent.

As I approached the final class of the day, I was a bit anxious because the teacher and I had definitely tangled the previous day and I had no idea how much she'd still be pissed with me. But clearly something had been said to her after we'd departed the previous afternoon, because she couldn't have been more friendly and welcoming to me.

"Welcome, Adam," she told me at the start of the class. "We are all delighted to have you joining our school and especially this class."

I nodded but didn't smile or give any other hint of emotion. She walked over to me in the back of the room and handed me a textbook along with a printed syllabus for the class.

"If you will stay after class this afternoon, I'd like to review with you what was covered yesterday so that you're caught up with everyone else."

"I can't. I have to take the bus home. I don't have a car, so the bus is my only way home, and it's way too far to walk."

I could tell she wasn't pleased with that answer, but she was doing her damnedest to be polite. "Absolutely not a problem," she cheerfully told me. "We'll find another time soon that works best for you, and I'll get you caught up with the rest of the class." Whatever the principal had said to her after yesterday's meeting must have been intense to bring about this total transformation of character. I was glad that everyone in the class was witnessing this happen.

I nodded in acknowledgement but otherwise kept my mouth shut.

I was at a complete disadvantage that afternoon, because I hadn't been in the class the previous day and didn't know what they'd talked about. I made a polite pest of myself throughout class, interrupting her repeatedly to ask questions or to request information I didn't have—obviously material she'd covered with everyone else the previous afternoon. But I didn't see an alternative—I had questions and I couldn't understand what she was talking about without asking my questions.

But I made sure to be unerringly polite. Apparently, though, I was polite in a way that didn't sit right. I gathered quickly that she objected to me calling her "ma'am."

"Adam, it's all right. You can use my name. You don't have to call me ma'am. I'm not that old."

"Excuse me, ma'am, but I don't know what your name is so I can't use it."

I couldn't decide if she was embarrassed or wanted to throw something at me. Whichever it was, she smiled and introduced herself, all of this during the middle of the class. "I'm so sorry, Adam. I keep forgetting that not everyone has lived in this community all their lives. My apologies. My name is Mrs. Hewitt." Once I had her name, I started to use that since I still had questions to ask.

As Ben had mentioned in the principal's office, there had been homework assigned the previous day. When she'd asked everyone to hand their homework forward, she told everyone that homework was a part of our grade and any assignments not completed and turned in would all count against our final grade in her class. The person in front of me turned around to collect mine, but I told him, "Sorry, I don't have anything," loud enough for everyone to hear.

Ben was seated at the front of the room, and I was seated at the back of the room, so after class he made it out of his seat and the room faster than I could. Also, I sat in my seat about thirty seconds longer than necessary, pretending to write something in my notebook to give Ben time to get ahead of me.

I saw Ben on the bus, but deliberately didn't sit with him, even though it would have been possible since there was an open seat right beside him. He looked up at me expectantly as I walked toward him. It nearly killed me, but I kept right on walking and sat instead with Bill. We talked and laughed, and I knew that Ben heard us because he kept turning to look our way all the way home. When we got to our stop, Ben got off first since he was closer to the front of the bus. He didn't hang around or wait for me but stomped directly off toward his own house while I headed to mine.

Now that school had started, I was no longer obligated to go help Ben work the fields and the barn during the week. I had homework to do and other things to keep me occupied. I knew I should probably have called him or gone over or something, but I wasn't in the mood to put on a smiling face and pretend that everything was fine. It was doubly difficult because I really wanted to see him, and even more I wanted to cuddle up next to him and feel him wrap his arms around me. It just sucked that our relationship seemed to have vanished like steam dissipating in dry air.

The rest of the week fell out the same way, settling down into an early and easy routine. I was very nervous the third day because Amelia was back. She'd been such a pain in my backside the first day and then gone the second day, but that third day she came back, and I didn't know how she would behave toward me. She clearly wasn't my biggest fan, but she didn't try anything. She was seated beside Ben in all of the classes because of the way she'd arranged things the first day, but at least that day she didn't have her hands all over him.

Ben and I were cordial but formal whenever our paths crossed, keeping each other at arm's length in public, which was just fine. One day at lunchtime, he went to an empty table, looking my way and discretely gesturing with his head for me to join him. I was going to, but before I could, the seats at his table were taken over with a whole bunch of rowdy guys who clearly knew Ben. Even though there was an empty seat at his table, it clearly wasn't my crowd, so I decided to go elsewhere, ending up sitting with Bill. I noticed that Ben kept looking my way, but I wasn't sure what he expected me to do.


THAT WEEKEND I was supposed to help Melinda in the road stand on Saturday morning. Then I was supposed to help Ben pick apples in the afternoon. I'd sort of expected that we'd talk while doing that work, but it turned out that we were just two out of about a dozen people hired to pick apples that day. Ben was in charge in some way, so he was busy running around, and we never had a chance to interact.

When my work was done, I left. Ben wasn't around, so I assumed he was busy elsewhere. So much for our chance to talk while we worked. That evening I almost hoped he wouldn't show up at our door because I was so tired and sore from all of the physical labor; all I wanted to do was take a bath and go to bed.

The next day I was pissed that Ben didn't call or come around. I missed him and wanted to see him. Hell, I still wanted to talk with him about the whole mess the first day of school to get his take on it. I really had expected him to show up that day, if for nothing else than to talk about what had happened at school.

I had so many questions. It wasn't like we lived twenty miles away. He could have come over. I wasn't going to reach out the first hand—I was waiting for him to make the first move.

Our second week of school presented us with a totally unexpected twist to our schedule. My dad usually went back to the city early one morning, spent the night, and drove back the next day, arriving back late at night.

But that week he had to change his plans. That week he made his trip back to the city first thing Monday morning and was planning to be gone for a full week, not returning until the following Sunday. This was the first time since we'd moved north into the middle of nowhere he was going to be away for such an extended period of time. He asked me if I wanted to stay with Melinda and Ben while he was gone, but I wasn't ready for that yet, so I told him no.

Ben knew I was home alone, but he was cautious around me that week. Several days he looked like he wanted to say something, but he didn't. A couple of days he actually worked up the nerve to speak to me, asking me how I was doing with my dad gone. I think it was the third day when he asked me if he could come over after school or in the evening. Prior to school starting, he would just show up. I really missed the old Ben.

It was a horrible coincidence that just when my dad was out of town and we could have spent many nights together in bed all night long, Ben and I were barely speaking. No way I was letting him spend the night—I was still too pissed with him about everything related to school. If he was expecting anything physical to happen he would be sorely disappointed. The first night this wasn't an issue, because I made it crystal clear that I wasn't in a cuddly kind of mood (I was, but I didn't let him know that). We sat on opposite sides of the room from each other and never touched—not once—not for any reason. We quietly watched television as if we were each the only person in the room while we each did our homework separately.

Before school had started, he'd told me repeatedly how we'd get together after school every day to do our homework, but those fantasies just never happened. We were in the same classes and had the same assignments, but I didn't feel the same drive to help him out with his homework. Maybe I was being bull-headed. Maybe I was being selfish. I didn't know.

The third night I couldn't take it anymore. Clearly Ben wasn't going to talk to me, so I decided enough was enough.

"Are we ever going to talk about anything?" I finally blurted out suddenly and forcefully.

"Like what?" he asked.

"Oh, I don't know, like maybe how all of the stuff we talked about before school started hasn't happened."

"What do you mean?"

"Quit being so damned difficult," I told him. "You know very well what I mean. We need to finish the conversation we started at the bus stop the second day of school. Before school started, we had this all planned out, but none of it is happening. It all went to hell in a hurry that first day." Ben looked down, even though I wasn't trying to make him feel guilty.

"Stop that," I told him.

"What?" He was confused.

"I didn't say that to make you feel guilty. I said it because I want to talk. I think we need to talk about all of this. We used to be able to talk. Hell, I used to see you. Since school started I don't feel like I ever see you. It's like I don't even know you anymore." I was quiet for a minute, debating with myself as to whether I should say the next part or not. What the hell. "I miss you." There. I said it.

"I miss you too," he shot right back, looking all vulnerable and lovable. "I hate how you've been mad at me."

"And I hate being mad at you. I've been really confused. I don't understand any of this, and I need you to help me sort it out. You haven't been there, and I've been a little scared."

"I'm really sorry about how this all worked out. Please believe me when I tell you I didn't plan it this way."

"I believe you."

"You do?" he asked.

"Yes. Is there some reason I shouldn't?" I asked him, suddenly curious.

"No. I just didn't know if you'd ever forgive me. You seemed so mad at me."

"I have been mad. I was pissed. I felt hurt. And I've felt so alone and lonely. You built it up to be one thing, and then not one bit of what you described came to pass. And on top of that you've been with 'that woman'"—as I'd taken to calling Amelia—"I've just been waiting for her to turn you against me completely."

The time for conversation was over. We were at the hugging stage. When Ben closed the distance that separated us and wrapped his arms around me, I sort of melted into his embrace.

"Do you know what the solution is?" I asked him after his hug.

"No. What?"

"Don't make me mad!" I practically yelled at him. At least he laughed. It had been forever since I'd heard him laugh. At last the ice was broken.

"I'm really sorry, Adam. Nothing went like I expected it that first day. I'm so sorry about that, but I was as caught off guard by everything that happened as you were."

"I kept looking to you all day long to help me figure out what the fuck was happening, but you wouldn't even look at me most of the time," I complained.

"I didn't have a clue what was happening so how could I help you—I was as lost as you were."

"Fine. I can understand that now. I have just one final question."

"Okay. Hit me with it," he told me as he took a deep breath as if preparing to go into a fight.

"Why the hell didn't you just tell Amelia no? That would have stopped everything."

"No, it wouldn't have. You don't know her. When she gets her mind set on something, nothing is going to come between her and what she wants. I couldn't have stopped her. I might have put her off for ten minutes or so, but she knew what she wanted, and she arranged just about everything as she wanted it that day. You were just a speed bump she hadn't expected. She still doesn't know what to make of you, or what to do with you."

"Let's hope it stays that way," I told Ben. "A healthy dose of caution isn't a bad thing on her part."

We were quiet for a moment, each grabbing glances at the other.

"I've missed you," I repeated my earlier statement. "I don't like being mad at you. And I don't like feeling so isolated and alone. You know all these folks, but I'm brand-new. I don't know anybody but you."

"You seem to be making friends with your science lab partner."

"Yeah, he's a great guy." And then, just to see if Ben was actually listening, I added, "And he's got one hell of a hot ass."

"Excuse me?" Ben asked, sitting up straighter in his chair. Yep, he'd been listening.

"You heard me."

"I don't want you checking out some other guy's ass," Ben told me.

"Fine. You got any other ass for me to check out?" It turned out he did. And I am happy to report that the substitute he had was a mighty fine example. Ben spent the night with me, and he apologized to me several times that evening, each one just a bit more personal and intense than the last. I did like the way he apologized.

# Chapter Eighteen
# Later That Fall

WE SETTLED into a routine over the weeks that followed with everything proceeding fairly quietly and uneventfully, much to my delight. My dad's one-week trip back to the city proved to be the start of a new pattern for us. He was involved with something big and was gone more than he was there with me. As September gave way to October, I had weeks at a time when I didn't see him. He kept in touch with me via e-mail and phone calls and had Melinda checking up on me all the time, but by early October, his trips to upstate were the exception as opposed to the rule.

For my part, I was doing just fine by myself. Ben and I were doing well once again, so I no longer felt so all alone and isolated. Melinda had me over to eat with them on a fairly regular basis. Or maybe I should say she extended an invitation to me on a regular basis. I wasn't there all the time. Sometimes I went most of the week without going over, but on the weekend, I'd spend most of my time at their house with Ben.

Things at school were okay, but Amelia was still a sore point for me. She wasn't grappling onto Ben all the time with her arms, but she was still somewhat possessive of him, keeping a constant eye on him when he was with me for even five minutes. We were both very much aware of the hawklike eye she kept on the two of us when we were together. With me she was polite but cold, which was fine because I had no desire to be her friend.

It was sometime around late October when I got a letter from Cornell University. I'd applied to their undergraduate program and was nervous as hell about it. Cornell was a top-notch school, and I knew that competition to get in was ferocious. And while I was a good student, I wasn't sure I was a good-enough student.

So when the envelope arrived in the mail, I was terrified to open it. It was either good news or really, really terrible news. Either way, it was going to be a big factor in where I went the next fall. After turning the envelope over and around, I laid it on the kitchen table and walked around it, looking at it from every angle, almost afraid to touch it.

I was afraid to open it, but I couldn't just leave it there on the table mocking me, so I grabbed it up quickly and practically ran over to Ben and Melinda's house. I needed Melinda and fortunately she was there.

Out of breath, I headed straight to her, bypassing Ben, and said, "Help."

"What's wrong?" she asked, looking so worried.

"Here," I told her. "This came today. I can't open it. I need to know, but it scares the crap out of me. It's too early for them to be admitting me, but they might be writing to reject me." I know I was babbling, but I couldn't stop. "My dad went there, so I'm what he calls a 'legacy' admission, and he said those are decided and announced first. This might be that, or it might be something else. I can't stand this. What if they don't want me? They're not going to want me. There are a whole lot of people that want every single spot they've got open. I don't stand a chance of getting in. I don't know why I even tried there. But it would be awesome if I did get in." I wanted to bang my head against a wall. "Make it stop! Please," I implored her.

She took the envelope from me and opened it, extracting the letter and reading it to herself for a moment before looking up at me. I was absolutely on a razor thin edge waiting for her to give me some sign of what they had to say. Each second longer that I had to wait I was just that much closer to falling absolutely to pieces.

Finally, she folded the letter back into its original arrangement and looked down. When she didn't look at me, I was convinced I was a worthless nothing. And then she broke into a huge grin and said, "You got in!"

To say that I was happy would be the understatement of the year. I jumped. She jumped. I cheered. She cheered. I was ecstatic. I hugged her. I hugged Ben. I hugged her again. And then I jumped around a bit more.

"I've got to go call my dad," I announced. "Thank you for doing that for me," I told her, referring to the opening of the letter. I took it with me and raced back to my house to call New York.

I was so happy in the days right after that, I completely missed the fact that Ben was slowly growing a bit more distant. He was still there, but I realized later that he was becoming more removed, a bit emotionally absent. It took me a couple of weeks to realize the extent to which this was true. I was so preoccupied with my excitement and with stuff I had going on at school that I completely missed it. He still came around occasionally, and we'd do homework and watch television. Once or twice we even had rattle-the-bedframe hot sex.

Things seemed to go well for the rest of October, but in early November I got a rather rude awakening. Out of the blue—to me, at least—we hit an unexpected speed bump. No, actually, I think this one was more of a pothole than a speed bump.

My dad was gone far more than he had anticipated, or at least more than he had let on to me. He had agreed to represent someone big in a major case back in the city, and I guess it was turning out to be a far more complex case than he had anticipated. So he was gone fully 95 percent of the time that fall. That fall he spent most of his time, including weekends, in his office in the city preparing for the big trial. I had no problem with that.

The problem unexpectedly arose on a Thursday night during the first week in November. I was lonely or bored or both, so I walked over to Ben's house to spend some time there just to hear some other people. I hadn't called first or asked Melinda if I could come over, but I figured that she'd given me a standing invitation, so it wouldn't be a problem for me to just show up at their door. I didn't do it all that often.

When I knocked at the door, Melinda answered.

"Hey, Adam. What are you up to?"

"Hi Melinda. I just walked over to see Ben for a few minutes."

"He's not here, baby."

"He's not?" That was a surprising bit of news since Ben was always there. Ben never went anywhere except to school. He was the original homebody.

"No. He's with Amelia again." I felt the blood drain from my face with those words.

"Excuse me?" I asked, hoping that the words made it out of my head. I guess they did because Melinda answered me.

"He's with Amelia. They're working on their science project together. Is that what you're working on tonight? They've been working hard on it for a couple of weeks now."

We didn't have any science project, so he'd given his mother a line of pure BS. It was only by chance that I'd stopped over that night, which made me wonder how many other things were going on that I didn't know about.

"Adam? Are you all right?" she asked, looking concerned.

"Oh, sorry. What?"

"Are you okay? You don't look so good."

"Yeah. Just kind of lonely I guess. It's really quiet over there all alone."

"Come on in. Watch some TV with me. You know I go to bed early, but you're welcome to stay and watch TV, or even to stay over. You know you're always welcome here. Don't ever forget that."

I was quite torn. Part of me wanted to stomp away back down the road to my house and bar the door never letting Ben in ever again, but another part of me liked the idea of spending some time with Melinda, and then catching him when he snuck in later.

"Maybe I'll watch TV with you for a couple of minutes," I told her. "When did Ben leave?" I asked, trying to gauge when he might be back.

"About five, I think." So he'd been gone a couple of hours already.

"Did he say when he'd be back?" I asked her, trying to sound casual.

"No, I don't think so, but the other times it's been late—after I went to bed."

I don't remember what we watched on TV that night. It didn't matter. It could have been anything because my mind was on anything but what was on the screen in front of me. I'd gotten there about seven thirty. She went to bed at nine, but I stayed, willing to give Ben a little bit longer. I really needed to know what was going on.

It was about nine forty-five when I heard the front door open and then close. "Mom, are you still up?" I heard Ben's voice as he walked into the room where I was sitting. He stopped dead in his tracks when he saw me, his eyes going open a great deal more than usual.

"How was your work on your science project?" I asked with a huge fake smile. "You get it all done? I hear you've been hard at work with Amelia for a couple of weeks now. You're such an industrious student. Your mom is so proud of you putting such an effort into your schoolwork. Too bad she actually believes that's what's going on."

His mouth opened as if to speak, but no sounds came out.

"Amelia must have blown you so good that she sucked your brains right out of your head. I guess that's why you've lost the ability to speak. At least I assume that's what's been going on, since we both know there is no science project."

I switched off the television using his mother's remote control and sat in the quiet room staring at Ben. We stared at each other for a good sixty seconds. I was waiting for Ben to say something, but he was frozen. He didn't move. He didn't speak. Finally, I was tired of waiting for him to make up a story because I knew that was all it would be— just a story. I stood up and started toward the door to head home. "Good-bye, Ben. Have a good life."

"Adam, wait, please," I finally heard as I reached the door. I stopped and turned back toward him, waiting to see what he had to say. It turned out to be nothing. He just looked at me with sad puppy dog eyes.

I turned to leave, feeling more alone than I had earlier in the afternoon. I got about ten feet away from the house before I heard the door open and quickly close again. In no time Ben was beside me. He didn't say anything, but he walked along beside me. Since I had a twenty-minute walk to get back to my house, he had lots of time to think of something to say.

We'd probably been walking for eight minutes when Ben suddenly said, "I'm sorry."

"I don't believe you," I told him.

"What can I say to make you believe me?"

"I don't have a fucking clue." I saw no reason to beat around the bush.

"You hate me, don't you?"

"You aren't exactly one of my favorite people right now. You see, I have this thing about not liking people who stab me in the back and lie to me."

"I deserve that."

"Damned right you do," I agreed.

We walked in silence for another minute when it was my turn to say something. "Have you been sleeping with her?"

He hesitated for a moment before trying to answer, which gave me all the answer I needed. "No," he finally said.

"Liar!" I yelled ferociously at him. "I don't believe you, Ben. You are the worst liar ever. I can't stand the dishonesty. I can't be with someone who doesn't even have the courtesy to tell me the truth. Go home, Ben, and leave me alone. I hope you and Amelia will be very happy together. Go fuck her some more and make a whole passel of kids. I can't do that for you. I hope you'll be happy with her and your life together."

I picked up the pace and moved ahead at a run, hoping he would take the hint and just leave me alone, which he surprisingly did. I will admit, a part of me wanted him to chase after me and beg me to forgive him, but a bigger part of me was glad he stopped and didn't try to say anything, because he was just going to fuck it up if he did.

I went home and went to bed, but I don't think I slept a bit that night. Cry, yes, but sleep, no. The next morning I just couldn't work up the ambition to get out of bed to go to school. I hadn't slept and I was too much of a wreck, so I just said fuck it. Who needed the drama? I finally got some sleep that morning, coming to about two in the afternoon. I thought I'd heard something but rolled over, convinced it was just something in a dream when I heard it again. There was someone at our front door.

Sluggishly I found some sweat pants and a T-shirt and pulled them on so I could go downstairs to see who was there. Wiping the sleep from my eyes, I opened the door to find Melinda on the other side.

"Adam, are you okay?"

"Sure. Why?" I asked.

"Ben called and told me you weren't in school. He was worried about you."

"Sure he was," I joked, but she didn't get it.

"Did you two have a fight of some sort?" she asked.

"Nope. He's a lying piece of crap, and I'm sick of it. That's all. No problem other than that." I stood staring at her, waiting for her to go away. I couldn't be mad at her—I liked her too much. Ben, on the other hand, I was less than fond of at that moment.

"I don't know what he's done, but I do know that he really likes you—a lot. I also know that he's scared about that."

"About what? About liking me?"

"Adam, I think we both know that it's more than like."

Did she really just say what I thought she'd said?

"He loves you. You know that. And he's terrified. He won't talk with me about it. If he would, I would tell him to follow his heart and live his life in a way that fulfills and pleases himself. You can't live your life concerned about what others think if you want to have any kind of a life."

"I believe you. Your son, however, he needs to hear you say that. And then he needs to stop sleeping with Amelia and lying to me about it." That appeared to be news to her—the sleeping with Amelia part.

"That boy is trying to straddle two worlds, and he's not doing very well in either."

"I can't believe I trusted him. Melinda, I really like you, which is why you need to leave, because I'm about this close to losing it, and I don't want to yell at you."

I didn't wait for her to say anything, but I just closed the door and went back upstairs to bed. Unfortunately, I didn't get back to sleep right away. The bed felt so good that I just stayed there. A couple of hours later I heard someone else knocking at our door. Since we didn't know that many people the odds were it was one of two people. It turned out that it was both of them. I found both Ben and his mom at my door.

"Yeah?" I asked, opening the door just enough to be able to speak to them. There was no way I was letting them in.

"I'm sorry," Ben told me again.

"Yeah, you've said that a lot this fall. Too bad for you that I don't believe it anymore."

"I know. But I really am sorry."

"For what?" I asked him. "For lying to me? Or for getting caught?"

"Both, but mostly I'm sorry for lying to you."

"Got it. Thanks for stopping by," I told him, intent on ending this conversation.

"It's rare for someone as great as you to come along," he said to me.

"I once thought the same way. I got over it. You clearly beat me to it."

"You're mad. I know it. You've got every right to be mad. I... I've been an idiot. I've been so scared."

He looked at me as if he expected me to say something, but I didn't have anything to say, so I just stood there and waited for him.

"You're from a different world than me. You're going places. You're going to go to college and make something of yourself. That means you'll be leaving here—and leaving me. And I'm not going anywhere. I'm where I want to be. I got scared when I thought of you moving on and me having to stay here without you. So I... I fell back on my safety net, to the only thing I knew."

I looked at him. That was the most words I'd had from Ben in a long while. And I believed him too.

"Why didn't you just talk to me?" I asked him calmly, catching him off guard.

"I didn't know how."

"Here's a clue—you open your mouth and speak words—like you've just done. It's that simple. I don't read minds, so unless you tell me, I don't know what's going on inside your head. I understand being scared. Trust me. I've been scared a whole lot over the last six months. But unless you actually open your mouth and tell me about it, I can't know about it, and I can't help you."

"I know. Wait. Help me?" he asked.

"Yes. Help you. I thought we were in this together."

Ben was still looking down, not meeting my gaze. "You hurt me, Ben. You really, really hurt me. When I heard you were with her, it meant not only had you lied to me, but it also meant I wasn't good enough for you, that I wasn't something that you wanted or needed. You'd tried me out and then discarded me. That's what I saw and heard by your actions."

"That's not it at all." Damn, now he had tears in his eyes. Well, I was just a goner. How could I possibly be mad at him with him showing so much vulnerability?

"How long have you been having sex with both of us?" I asked him.

"A few weeks," he answered me. "Two, maybe three weeks."

"Have you been using condoms with her?"

He hesitated. Oh, this was not going to be good. "Most of the time."

"Most of the time," I parroted back to him, not believing what I was hearing. "Most of the time? Ben, we didn't use condoms when you and I were together, and now I find out that I've made a horrible mistake. I thought I could trust you, Ben. I thought I could trust you to be concerned about my health and well-being, and now you tell me that my trust was misplaced. I trusted you to keep me and my health safe. Well, talk about a kick to the gut."

I didn't know what to say now. My brain was working, but it didn't seem to be coming up with anything to help me. Finally, some words came to me.

"I will tell you right here and now that if you've picked up something from having unprotected sex with her and passed it on to me, I will come to your house in the dark of night and whack your nuts off with a machete. Do you hear me?"

He nodded, a few tears still in evidence.

"I'm so sorry," Ben returned to his original mantra.

"So what happens now?" I asked him.

Finally, something that made Ben look up at me. He looked right at me as he told me, "I've broken it off with her. I've told her point blank I cannot see her anymore and that I do not love her and never have and never will."

I nodded. "I bet she loved hearing that."

"She wasn't especially happy," he agreed, "but to go on deceiving her was just going to make it that much worse. Just like deceiving you was only going to make things worse. I do hope that someday you'll be able to forgive me for being so scared. I'm not strong like you are."

"You've got that backwards. I'm not the strong one—you are," I told him.

"I've missed you so much. And then the thought of you sitting here all alone is this big old empty house, hurting, just about broke my heart today. All I can ask is that you please don't hate me. You're one of a kind, Adam. You're my first."

"Your first what?"

"The first guy I've ever loved. The first guy I've ever had sex with. The first guy I've ever wanted to spend the rest of my life with."

"Is that all?" I joked.

"Yeah, just some little stuff." He tried to match my mood.

I looked at Melinda for some guidance. She smiled and nodded at me. I pushed the front door open and told the two of them, "Get in here. It's cold out there."

We had tea and sat in our kitchen for hours talking that afternoon.

"Ben," I started. "Here, read this," I told him, handing him an envelope.

"What is it?" he asked, looking confused.

"Open it!" I ordered. "Read it."

He pulled the letter from the envelope and read it.

"It's your acceptance letter to Cornell. Yeah. I know all about it. This is what got me into such a panic in the first place. Why are you showing me this?"

"Think, Ben."

"About what?"

Good Lord. Was I going to have to take him by the hand and lead him to where I wanted him? "Where is Cornell?"

"It's in Ithaca."

"Jesus, you are being stubborn today," I bitched at him. "And where is Ithaca from here?"

"About thirty miles that way," he answered, pointed to the east.

I rolled my eyes. "And thirty miles is driving distance from here."

"You mean… you mean you could come back to… to what?"

"Sometimes I want to smack you in the head, Ben. It means I can stay here and drive back and forth each day for class if I want to. We could be together every day."

"Don't joke about something like that," he told me.

"I'm not joking," I told him.

"But why would you want to drive back and forth when it would be so much easier for you to live on campus like all the other students?"

"Simple. You." It was a toss-up as to which of them was going to lose it first, Ben or his mother. "But we have to get some things straight first."

"Okay. What?" he sounded eager.

"If we're doing this—you and me—I want it to be just that—you and me. No one else, ever. Understood? Any objections? If so, spit it out now."

"I understand. I only want to be with you. You're all I need."

"So, no one else?"

"No one else," he promised with a huge smile.

"If I ever find out that you've lied to me like you did this time, there will be a holy wrath like nothing you've ever seen before. You'll try to run, but there is nowhere you'll ever be able to hide, because I will hunt you like a rabid animal. Are we clear?"

"Yes, Adam. I understand, and I agree. But I need the same promise from you."

"I think it's pretty obvious how important this is to me, but yes, absolutely, I promise."

"I'm the only man for you? Ever?"

"You're my only man."

Ben was beaming. "It's like we just got married," he bragged.

"In many ways, yes, it's exactly like that. We just made vows to one another. Your mother was our witness. It may not be legal, but consider yourself quasi-married."

"You two need to talk. I'll go home and get dinner ready. Come on over when you're ready. We'll eat in an hour."

And suddenly we were alone, and we could tackle the tougher issues. I took a deep breath before addressing the next part. "If you just broke it off with Amelia, she's going to be pissed, and she's going to be gunning for me like never before. I need your help this time in dealing with her."

"You've got it."

"I thought I had it last time, too, but it turned out I didn't. Last time you just sat and watched and let it happen right before your eyes. You didn't look at me. You didn't talk to me. You didn't help me. You hung me out to dry. I can't do that again. This time I need your active participation in helping to go up against her. Can you do that?"

"Yes, Adam, I can do that."

"I know you can, but will you do that?"

"Yes," Ben looked me right in the eye and promised, "I will do that. I'm happy, Adam."

"Well, wait one minute. You may not be when you hear my final point."

"Okay. Go ahead," Ben told me.

"Since you've been with her, we cannot be together... sexually... until some time has passed and we've both gone to a doctor and been tested for a whole range of sexually transmitted diseases. If, and only if, we both get clean bills of health from the doctor based on those tests, then we can talk about resuming our sex life—but not until."

Ben looked down. I was guessing he was embarrassed for having introduced this huge kink into our relationship. His gaze moved back up, and he looked right at me. "I understand. Except for the first couple of times, which happened unexpectedly, I used a condom—when I was with her. I understand your concern. Yes, absolutely, of course I'll go with you to the doctor and get tested."

"After we've given it a couple of weeks for anything you might have picked up to become evident we'll go. And before then, I want you to tell me if anything is weird. Like if you have a burning sensation in your dick when you pee, since that means you've got something. Like if you have unexplained pain anywhere. You got it? Anything. I want to hear all of it."

"I can't touch you for how many weeks?" he sort of whined in a most unbecoming fashion.

"I'm guessing it will be three to four weeks."

"A whole month? Jesus, that's like forever."

"Almost," I told him. "But those are my terms. Take it or leave it."

"I take it," he unhappily muttered.

"You agree?" I asked. I needed to hear the words.

"I agree."

Since that covered my big issues, and it was nearly time for dinner, I went upstairs to take a shower and get dressed. I was surprised to walk out my front door twenty minutes later to find Ben waiting for me. He smiled that smile of his that got me every time.

"What are you doing out here in the cold? It's freezing out here."

"Waiting for you, so I could do this." He stepped beside me and took my hand in his. We walked hand in hand to his mother's house.

And I was happy. Ben had never held hands outdoors with me before—I liked it.

We had dinner with Melinda, and then, because their house was warmer than ours ever was, I stayed over. Rather than return to my empty, cold house, I crawled into Ben's bed and slept there that night. I didn't crawl into his bed to fuck him. I wanted something more—I wanted to cuddle with him.

We didn't do anything physical, and in fact we both kept our underwear on, but we were together and we cuddled, enjoying the comfort of touching one another and the mere presence of the other.

# Chapter Nineteen
# Unexpected Visitor

IN THE days that followed, Ben was the most attentive lover any man could ever ask for—if the term "lover" works in a nonsexual relationship, that is. Of course, nothing physical was going on as we had agreed, unless you considered snuggling, holding hands, and lots of cuddling to be "something."

He was by my side constantly, smiling at me, holding my hand when we were alone, and most important he was talking to me. When he told me he got scared, I did what I could.

"We all get scared Ben. I've been scared too. It's not like we have examples we can look at, like everybody else has, of what a gay couple is supposed to be, or look like, or how we're supposed to act." And it was true—we didn't know any gay couples who could be our models of what we were supposed to do. We didn't have any mentors, just when we most could use such a thing.

As I had anticipated, Amelia, who was already not my most favorite person, became something approaching my all-time worst enemy since Ben was now spending all of his time with me instead of her. She didn't know the nature of our relationship, but she saw me beside Ben instead of herself. She and her entire band of bitches were constantly whispering about me when they knew I could hear. They spread all kinds of rumors about me, half of which I completely disregarded. The other half pissed me off so much I was fuming.

But we took it day-by-day. Ben asked our science teacher if he could switch seats with me, but I told him no. I liked working with Bill, and I didn't want him to get stuck with Amelia. I just couldn't do that to the guy. I did, however, agree to switch seats with her in some of our other classes. Most of the teachers didn't give him any problem when he'd asked; our homeroom teacher did give him some pushback, but Ben pushed right back, politely of course, and finally got the guy to relent.

If she had disliked me before, Amelia just plain outright hated me after that. But I didn't especially care, since she didn't get to define who I was—I was the only one who got to do that. All in all, her opinion didn't count for anything with me. I did my level best to be constantly cordial, to even smile at her—partly because I knew it pissed her off so much. After a whole lot of sneering and scowling my way, she finally settled down and moved to just ignoring me. That I could deal with.

It got especially better when she started to go out with one of the football players. After that, I basically didn't even register with her, which was just fine with me.

We started alternating, one night Ben spent the night at our house, and then the next I'd spend the night at his house sleeping in his bed. We were still just cuddling since I wasn't ready to resume the physical part of our relationship. I'd insisted that we wait a couple of weeks, see a doctor to get tested for things, and then, if we were clear, I'd consider resuming the physical part. I couldn't tell him this, but I really wanted him. Cuddling with him, feeling his strong arms around me at night was one of the most erotic things any gay man could ask for. I wanted to strip those shorts off him and make him—and me—feel good, but I didn't. I waited. It was important to wait.

It was the Saturday before Thanksgiving when the world exploded. Well, not the entire world, but my little part of it did, giving me a major sense of déjà-vu. I hadn't seen my dad in weeks since his trial in the city was dragging on and on and on. So you can imagine my surprise when I woke to find him standing in my bedroom staring at me—or more properly at us, since Ben was firmly wrapped around me from behind.

He didn't say a word but turned and left the room.

"Ben, wake up! My dad just saw us. Quick, get dressed."

By the time we were dressed, we saw him stalking down the driveway. I knew instinctively where he was headed, so Ben and I raced out of the house and took off after him. We never did quite catch up, but we were just a few seconds behind him.

Melinda's vegetable market was doing gangbuster business that day since it was the last Saturday before Thanksgiving. Everyone wanted to have the freshest, most natural stuff with which to prepare their holiday feasts. She'd told me that it was her busiest day of the year with everybody wanting apples for pies, squash for roasting, pumpkins for pies, to name just a few of the many things she sold. When I saw the crowd, I believed her. I wondered why she'd told us she didn't need us there until noon when it was already so busy. I later learned that someone hadn't shown up for work and that she'd been about to call us when all hell broke loose.

My dad apparently didn't see the many people in the market, because he stormed up to Melinda while she was in the middle of something and just started yelling at her.

"I asked you to watch my son, and what do I find when I get back here? *Your* son in bed with him. Is that what you call watching out for someone's child?"

"Dad, you're making a scene in public," I pleaded. "Not now, please. And I'm not a child—I'm a man."

"You are only seventeen years old. You're not old enough to know what you want. I should probably call the police and have Ben arrested. I think that's exactly what I should do."

"Dennis!" Melinda yelled at him to get his attention. "You'll do no such thing. This is not the time or the place, as your son tried to tell you. You're making a scene in front of the entire community. Is that what you really want to do?"

A number of people who had been shopping for vegetables for their Thanksgiving feasts stopped what they were doing to pay attention to the major ruckus my dad was causing. I noticed a number of folks move to Melinda's side, standing with her.

One woman went so far as to tell my dad, "Sir, I don't know who you are, but you are not acting like a responsible adult. As Melinda told you, this is not the time or the place to discuss a private family matter. Might I suggest that you take your conversation outside—and also lower your voice and keep in mind that everyone here loves Melinda and has known her for years and thinks she is the best. If you attack her, then you are attacking all of us, and we country folk stand together against bullies like you."

"Bully? Is that what you think I am?" he demanded.

"Sure seems right to me," she told him. "You come rushing in here on a crowded, busy day yelling at this poor woman. I gather that you asked Melinda to do your job and watch over your child. I don't know you or your child, but I can tell you Ben is one of the finest young men I know, and his mother has raised a good one with him."

"Who the hell are you and why are you talking to me?" he angrily demanded.

"I'm Melinda's friend, and I'm talking to you because you've started yelling at my friend in a very public way, and I do not like it. I'm standing with my friend since you are scaring all of us."

That seemed to shock my dad back into reality. He took a step back and then surprised me. "I'm sorry, Melinda. You're right. This isn't the time or the place. We need to talk."

"All right, Dennis, but I can't right now. This is one of my busiest days of the year. When I close tonight I can. Can this wait?"

"I suppose." He exited the store much more quietly than how he had entered.

"Is that the man who owns the Caldwell farm?" Melinda's defender asked.

"Yes. That's him."

"What an asshole," she summed it up before returning to her shopping.

Since it was so busy, Ben and I stayed and pitched in to help keep things moving, to check customers out, and to help them get their heavy things to their cars. We earned a couple of bucks in tips, which I was guessing I was going to need soon. If my dad's prior behavior was any indication, I was guessing he was going to want to move again— who knew where—in his quest to "save" me. Only this time I had a surprise for him—I wasn't going anywhere.

If it meant that Ben and I had to leave, had to hit the road and just disappear, then that was exactly what I was willing to do. If he was going to have Ben arrested, then I was going to have to get Ben out of there since there was no way I was going to let that happen. But we hadn't been doing anything other than sleeping. There hadn't been any sex. All he'd seen was sleep, and surely that couldn't be a crime.

During one tiny lull I pulled Melinda aside and asked her an important question. "Do you think he meant what he said, about having Ben arrested?"

"I don't think he can. At least I certainly hope not," she told me with less conviction than I was hoping.

"We were only sleeping. Nothing was happening. We were both sound asleep when he came in." I looked at her, feeling desperately afraid of what was going to happen. "We need to get Ben out of here," I told her. "I can't have him arrested. He hasn't done anything."

She sighed, looked away for a moment, deep in thought.

"All right."

She turned to Ben and called him over to where we were standing. "Honey, I need you to do something for me. Can you do that? Please."

"Sure, Mom. Of course. What?"

"I need you to go take my truck and go see your Aunt Brenda."

"Why?" he asked, confused.

"Don't ask. Just go. Now. Please."

"You... you want me to hide?"

She looked at him and nodded. "Yes. That's what I want."

"I can't run away and hide."

"Please, Ben. Just for a few hours. Let us go up there and talk with Adam's father and see where we stand. We'll call you and let you know what happens. Please."

She held the keys to her truck out for him. I didn't think he was going to do it, but he took them and slowly walked out of the shop.

"Wow. I didn't think he'd do it," I told her.

"Neither did I. But I'm glad he did."

We dealt with another hour of business and then, as soon as we had closed down and locked up everything, we walked to her house. As we approached the house, we both spotted my dad sitting on the front steps.

"Oh God," I muttered. "This is not going to be fun."

"Just remember," Melinda told me, "you are not in this alone this time."

"Thanks. You don't know how much that helps me."

"Oh, I think I have a good idea," she said as we closed the distance that separated us.

Nothing was said beyond pleasantries until we were all in the kitchen sitting around the table.

"I was rather surprised," my dad started, "to come back here this morning and find Ben in bed with Adam."

"They were sleeping, Dennis. That's all. Sleeping," Melinda told him, beating me to it by a second.

But she wasn't finished. "They love each other, Dennis. You've been too busy, too absent, too distant to see, but they've loved each other for many, many months, long before you went away. Their relationship started nearly six months ago."

"You knew about this?" he asked, sounding incredulous.

"Not at the time, no. But now I do. You see, my approach to parenting is not like yours. I don't yell at my kid and throw around a lot of accusations and demands. I talk with him. In fact, I've had some great talks with both Adam and Ben, separately and together. They are two fine young men."

When she saw my dad start to shake his head, she reiterated her point. "Yes, Dennis, they are men. Our little boys have grown up. As hard as it is for a parent to realize that their little boy isn't their little boy anymore, we need to be proud of the men they've turned into. Adam is a great man, and Ben is also a great man. They love each other, and if you had been here, you would know a little about the horrible roller coaster they've been on this fall.

"Did I know they were sleeping together? Yes. Are they having sex? No, not right now. They have had sex, starting nearly five months ago while you were here every day. From the look on your face, I see that you find this surprising. If you treat your son like a man and talk with him, you might know some of these things because he'd maybe be willing to come talk to you if he knew you weren't going to yell at him." She paused for a moment before continuing. "Dennis, I've only known you for a few months, but it's enough to tell me that you are a good man, a good father, a bit stubborn and pigheaded, but that just means you fit right in here," she said, joking a little to lighten the mood. I was pleased to see that it was working.

"We have two fine young men as sons. Our sons have fallen in love. I, for one, am pleased and proud of them, separately and together, because they've had a tough time this fall, but they've come through it stronger than ever. You don't have the first clue about what they've had to go through. Be proud of Adam, Dennis. Be proud of him. And for goodness' sake, don't try to run away with him again. There's nothing wrong with our sons. There's no need to run away because the 'problem' as you see it is just part of who they are. I love my son just as he is, as he was born. He's the man he was born to be. And so is your son. Be proud of him." She smiled at him.

At least he nodded at her comment.

"Now, earlier you spoke about having Ben arrested—"

"I'm sorry about that," he offered. "I'm not going to do that. They didn't break any laws that I know of. I shouldn't have threatened that."

"Good," she said, looking visibly relieved.

"I have one final point that you probably are not going to want to hear. This is the one that actually has me most concerned—no, worried, fearful. You really, really don't want to do again what you did this morning. I can guarantee you that what you said this morning has already been repeated and spread from one end of our valley to the other several times over since then. Country folk love gossip, and, Dennis, you gave them a bushel basket full this morning. I just hope we can all handle the fallout from what you've started, because I can guarantee that just about everyone around has now heard some variation on the story."

My father visibly blanched. He clearly had not realized this fact. I was suddenly scared, because it meant that my father had in effect just outed Ben and me, and when we went back to school on Monday, potentially everyone there would know that we had been caught sleeping together. Oh, this was not going to be good.

All the time we'd been talking, Melinda's phone had been ringing constantly. She'd been ignoring it, but she finally grabbed one of the calls when she'd said what she had to say. It was obvious that the call was from someone who had heard about what had happened that morning. We could only hear one side of the conversation.

"Yes, Margaret, you heard right. Ben is gay, and he's in love. Yes, they've been together for months." Pause. "Yes, I've known. Why wouldn't I approve? They're two fine young men, and I'm proud of both of them. I couldn't ask for a better son-in-law than Adam." She smiled at me as she said those words. I suddenly sat up straighter, feeling proud, which chased away all of my fears about being outed.

My dad went home, telling us that he needed some time to think. I called Ben to come home and was so relieved when he finally walked through the door. I spent the night at Ben's house in bed with him, because I didn't want to go home, afraid of what my dad might try next.

It was sort of background given the drama of the day, but we'd both received phone calls from the doctor we'd visited, giving both of us reports that were clean of any sexually transmitted diseases or any other of a host of things. With that news, when we went to bed that night, we could once again be lovers. The only problem was that we were both too stressed to even think about that.

# Chapter Twenty
# Coffee and Surprises

THE FOLLOWING morning we woke to find Ben's mom and my dad sitting together in the kitchen over cups of coffee. My dad, the one who was not a morning person, was up, dressed, and looking rather alert for such an early hour of the day. When he spotted us, my dad made the first move.

"Morning, Adam. Morning, Ben."

"Morning, Dad. You're up early."

"Unfortunately. I've got to hit the road and get back to the city for this damned trial I'm trapped with."

I had to make conversation so I asked, "So it's turned out to be different than you had planned?"

"Way beyond anything I could have imagined. I'm not happy. I'm supposed to be up here with you, keeping you out of trouble."

"I'm able to do that on my own, Dad. Don't worry about me."

"It's a father's job to worry." He paused for a moment. "But I know that you've got some really good folks who are here for you. Melinda, Ben, my thanks to both of you for everything you've done to take care of my son."

I thought he was done, but he surprised me. "Ben, I will not lie to you. I do not understand the appeal of two guys together. I just don't get it. But I suppose you don't see the appeal of a woman the way I do either." Ben kept his mouth shut. "I don't understand, but I want to try to learn a little since it's important to you two. I'm not going to get there overnight. Not gonna happen. It may take me years, but I am going to try."

"I'll give you a hand with that," Melinda told him.

"Ben, are you and my son sexually active together?" my dad asked. My heart sank.

"Yes, sir, we are. He's my boyfriend. We love each other," Ben answered him directly. The man had a big set of balls, I'll give him that. It took all of them to answer my dad directly like that.

My dad nodded and then turned to me. "Adam, do you love him? Does he treat you right?"

"Yes, Dad. I love him. And he treats me really well. And besides, if he doesn't, I just let him know. I'm not shy about those things."

He chuckled lightly. "I keep forgetting that you're a New Yorker at heart and you've got the balls to go with it."

"And I'm your son," I added softly. He didn't say anything, but from the smile on his face, I think I said exactly what he needed to hear me say.

As fast as it started, our moment was finished. "I've got to get on the road, or I'm going to miss my flight."

"Flight? Where are you flying?" I asked. He always drove.

"I'm flying back to the city. Since I'm tied up so much, I decided I needed to leave the car up here for you. I don't like the idea of you being stuck up here with no way to get around, no way to go buy groceries, or things like that. And I've dumped enough of my responsibilities on Melinda already. She's done it all without complaint, so it's time to free you up and take some of the burden off her. Remember, though, that the car is not a toy. Winter will be here any day now, and you don't know much about driving on ice or snow. If it looks bad, it is bad, and you just stay off the road. Leave the driving to those who know how to handle winter driving."

"Really? That's awesome. Thanks." To say I was excited would be an understatement. This was beyond awesome. To have wheels of my own at my disposal meant so much. It meant no more begging rides to the grocery store. And even more importantly, it meant no more school bus.

"Do you want to come home for Thanksgiving?" he asked suddenly.

I looked around the table at Melinda and at Ben, both of whom were utterly blank, not giving me a single hint of how they felt about the issue.

"No. I think I'll stay here, if I won't be in the way." The blank looks instantly transformed into approving looks.

"What about Christmas?" he asked.

"I'll think about it and let you know. I think I like the idea."

"Oh, and Ben, you should probably come to visit in December as well. My wife will want to meet you, and Adam can show you around the city a little. I understand you've never been there."

"That's right, sir. I've never been anywhere, really."

"Well, I'm sure Adam will want to show you lots of things. That boy does love to travel. I've got to get going," he announced as he stood up and grabbed his coat. Melinda drove him to the airport, which left us to our own devices to get ready for the day. Fortunately it was a low-key day.

The following morning I used the car to drive us to school, so our trip was fairly fast and uneventful. I hadn't driven in so long that I needed a few miles to get used to it again, to remember how it felt. We were both feeling really upbeat about the way things had turned out with my dad. We'd gone to bed expecting the worst and woke to find exactly the opposite. I needed to remember to thank Ben's mom, because I was sure she had a hand in it.

That week, the week of Thanksgiving, was an abbreviated week for us. We had school Monday and Tuesday as usual, but only a half day on Wednesday, and then, of course, we were closed for the remainder of the week. That morning we had lots to feel good about as we ditched our coats in our lockers. How quickly that changed.

We'd barely hung up our coats when I heard a male voice ask loudly, "So, Taylor. I hear you're queer now. Did the city boy turn you into a pussy? Are you his bitch, or is he yours?"

I gasped in shock at the words I'd just heard. This was bad. This was so, so bad. I turned around from my locker, which was a short distance from Ben's, to see a group of about six guys clustered around him. I didn't know any of them, but it looked like Ben knew most of them. Ben had his arms crossed over his chest and was projecting all kinds of confidence and assurance.

"Doolittle, what the hell are you talking about?" Ben demanded of him, looking and sounding once again like his old confident, intimidating self. The other guys were all good-sized, but Ben was the tallest of them, and he had the muscles he'd earned from long hours of working on the farm.

"You heard me. Do you and that city boy get naked and nasty now?"

"Why? You want in on it? Is that your way of asking me out on a date?" Ben asked.

"What the fuck, dude! No way! I'm no pussy. And I didn't know you were, either."

"I'm just me," Ben told him. "I'm the same guy you've known since the first grade."

"Bull, man. The guy I knew didn't suck some other guy's dick."

"I'll say it again," Ben told him. "I'm the same guy I've always been, the same guy you've known for most of your life."

"What does that mean?" Doolittle demanded of Ben.

"Just what I said. I'm the same guy I've always been. There's nothing different about me now."

"Bull. If you suck dick, that's a hell of a big difference."

"Hey, moron," one of the other guys in the circle interrupted Doolittle. "I think he's saying that he's always liked dick. Is that true, Taylor? You been checking us all out in the locker room? You been checking out our asses in the showers? Do we all need to ask the coach to keep you out of the showers?"

"Don't even think about it," Ben told them. "Just because you're guys—I think—doesn't mean I automatically want you. I've seen all of your asses, and let me tell you, you've got nothing to worry about from me. None of you have what I'm after."

"What's wrong with us?" another guy asked, which earned him stern looks from his buddies.

The bell telling us it was time to head to homeroom saved us. At least I hoped we were saved. My fear was that we weren't so much saved as we were just postponing the inevitable. We were in a rural area, not a demographic most noted for tolerance and acceptance. And in that setting, we'd just been outed by my father. I had to remember to thank him for that the next time I saw him. This might even make a phone call necessary.

Throughout the day people kept looking at both of us weirdly. Several times I saw people looking at one or the other of us, clearly talking with their friends about us. Of course, we couldn't hear what they were saying. I was sure that we would when they were ready to take it up a step. Thankfully, though, we got through that day. Although as we were exiting the building to head for the car, I heard someone yell, "Faggots!"

When I got home that night, I was so pissed that I did call my dad. He sounded stressed, but that couldn't be helped. I had stress to add to his stress.

"Adam, what's wrong? This isn't a good time."

"What's wrong? Oh, not much. I just wanted to thank you for outing Ben and me to the entire community. That would be the same community that all of our classmates come from."

"Oh crap. Did they give you trouble?"

I laughed. "What? Teenagers be mean? I've never heard of such a preposterous idea."

I heard him sigh. "I'm sorry," he said more softly than he usually spoke. "Do you want to come home?"

He had no way of knowing how much I wanted to go home, but he also didn't seem to understand that that was no longer an option. "That would work for me, but that doesn't do anything to solve Ben's problem. You outed him too. He's the one who got the brunt of it today. He's known all those kids his whole life. They turned on him today like a pack of jackals."

"Crap. I can't come back there now. This is... it's just too crazy here right now."

"I don't want you to come back here. The last time you did gave us troubles to last a lifetime." I know I shouldn't have done it, but I hung up on him. I was so pissed, and I wanted to hurt him. With my dad, I'm not sure that was possible, but what the hell, I had to give it a shot. Somewhere beneath that tough, crusty, miserable man, there had to be a heart. At least I hoped there was still one there somewhere.

Tuesday was brutal. Everybody was ready to be on vacation for a long weekend for Thanksgiving. No one was enthused about paying attention to anything the teachers were trying to cover. A lot of kids were mentally disconnected already as they were probably thinking about trips they were going to be making the following day to head off to see some relative or another. And what do bored teenagers do? That's right. They cause trouble.

Anytime we were moving between classes that day, it seemed like someone was after Ben or me. He got shoved more times than I could count. Ben's not a small guy. He was more than six feet tall with muscles. People needed to be careful about poking that bear, because when he got riled up, that bear could fight back and do some serious damage. So far Ben had taken the high ground and had quietly let people have their fun. I knew he had a limit. The only question was when that limit would be reached. I did not honestly know, but I knew that it would not be pretty when it happened.

I was no ninety-eight pound weakling, but I didn't have Ben's height and weight, so I didn't make quite so imposing a threat as he did. I guess that made me an easier target than Ben. The times that Tuesday when we were separated were the most dangerous times for me. The minute I was alone and he wasn't around to help me, the pack seemed to try to cut me off and herd me into danger zones. The first time I figured it out and didn't let them do it, but the second time I got cornered—of course out of view of any teacher, wouldn't you know.

One of the slower, bulkier students (he would really hate it if he knew I thought of him that way) advanced on me with an angry look on his face. The fact that I was completely surrounded by classmates didn't provide me one iota of help or protection. Just as Big and Bulky was getting within striking distance, something happened that caught all of them (me too, for that matter) off guard. Bill, my science lab partner, pushed his way through the ring of students and stood beside me. He didn't just stand there. He looked at the one coming at me and said simply, "Back off."

It took the guy a couple of seconds to decide how to handle this affront. I didn't think it was going to end well for us, so you can imagine my surprise when they actually did what Bill told them to do. When the crowd had dispersed, I asked him one question. "How did you do that?"

"Simple," he told me. "They used to pick on me all the time and made my life a living hell. They don't pick on me anymore—since I took self-defense training. I go to a karate dojo four times a week. I'm a brown belt working toward my black belt. They know I can kick their asses from here to next Tuesday and back again."

I laughed. Without thinking I hugged Bill. Quickly realizing what I had done, I said, "I'm sorry. I shouldn't have done that. I didn't mean any offense."

"Why would I be offended?" he asked me with a big smile.

"Really? You haven't heard all the gossip about me? About me and Ben?"

"Yeah? So?"

"I'm gay. I'm sure you don't want the gay guy hugging you."

"Do you really think you're the only gay guy in this school?" Bill asked me. The idea had absolutely never occurred to me that there were others. None of them had given me even so much as a hint about being gay, so I hadn't thought about it. Bill's news was astonishing to me.

"Don't act so surprised," he cautioned me.

"I'm sorry. I really *am* surprised."

"You shouldn't be. Everybody used to tell the new folks so they could be sure to steer clear of me."

"Never heard a word," I told him.

"Well, maybe I'm finally past that nightmare."

"Yeah, because now they have me and Ben to go after."

"Ben's a big guy. He should be able to take care of himself. You, however, they're gonna go after you every chance they get. You better stick with me as much as possible if you want to survive without major damage."

"Thank you," I told him, and I meant it from the bottom of my heart. "I… thank you."

"You're welcome. Consider it my community service to my gay community, which is now a community of three instead of just one." In the span of five minutes, I had gone from scared to terrified to relieved to happy. I liked the happy part.

# Chapter Twenty-One
# A Reason to Give Thanks

BEN AND I got through the following half day of school super easy, and by noon we were back in my dad's SUV, and I was driving us home. We had to stop at the grocery store to pick up a couple of things for Melinda, and of course it seemed like everyone had heard about us. Some people stood and stared, but most were more or less their usual selves. It gave me hope.

Melinda, Ben, and I had a wonderful Thanksgiving—one of the best I can remember ever having. We all cooked together and had a blast. Clean up wasn't so much fun, but even that wasn't too bad with the three of us working together. We spent the afternoon following our huge dinner watching movies and laughing.

The day after Thanksgiving, while Melinda shopped, Ben and I went out for a long walk through the woods. It was cold, even though the sky was clear blue and the sun was bright overhead.

The trees that just a month earlier had been filled with leaves of beautiful colors were now mostly bare. A few hardy stragglers hung on, but their days were numbered. Mother Nature had tucked the living things in for their long nap through the dark, cold days of winter. While we hadn't had snowfall yet, I knew it was only a matter of time before it started.

While we walked slowly beside each other that beautiful but cold fall day, Ben, the man of few words, surprised me by sharing some powerful ones with me.

"You know, this Thanksgiving was different for me."

"Why's that?" I asked him.

"Simple. This year I really had something to be thankful for."

"What? Surviving the week without getting into a fight?" I joked.

"No. For you."

Any hint of joking vanished. "For me? Really?"

"Really."

"You aren't sick of all the upset I've brought to your life?"

"Nope. I'm happy for all the joy you've brought into my life."

"You aren't mad because my dad outed us to the entire community?"

"I am, but I'm mad at him, not you. You didn't do that—that was all his doing."

"True," I agreed. "So that means that you, what? Kind of like me?" I joked with him.

"Maybe a little," he agreed, smiling as he squeezed my hand. "I've never been happier than I am right now—than I am with you," Ben told me.

"Wow. You don't talk a lot, but when you do, damn, you do it really well."

"Thank you," he told me with one of his own unique smiles. I don't know how he did it, but Ben smiled not just with his mouth, but somehow with his eyes as well. His whole face changed appearance to a certain degree when he smiled, when he was happy. It gave me great joy to know that I had done that. I felt like I was performing an important public service by getting Ben to smile. I know it made me feel a lot warmer and happier.

That afternoon, while his mother shopped, we snuggled in his bed, napping, playing, exploring. Ben wasn't the only one who had much to be thankful for that year. I was right there with him on that.

Was every day after that going to be smooth sailing? Hell no. I knew the days ahead would not all be easy, and that there would be some that probably just plain sucked, but we'd get through them. We'd do it together.

Who would have guessed that something that started out so horribly as getting caught in bed with your best friend could turn around so totally and guide you straight into the arms of the man you loved? I hadn't seen that coming. It had been a complete surprise to both of us, and in my view, the best surprises were the unexpected ones. Looking back, I was glad I'd gotten caught.

# Coming Soon
## Caught in the Act: Book Two

# *Caught in the Middle*

## By Robbie Michaels

After a rocky start to the school year, Ben and Adam are getting their feet on solid ground, despite a lot of obstacles. Amelia, Ben's former girlfriend, isn't willing to let Ben go so easily. At Christmas, Amelia delivers a bombshell that keeps Adam and Ben apart over the holiday. When Adam returns from seeing his family, Ben, who avoids conflict at all cost, will not talk to him.

Adam figures out Amelia's scheme, and when he confronts her, she retaliates by arranging an ambush in the school parking lot one night.

Ben is horrified when he sees Adam lying battered in the hospital. Adam is more than physically broken. His spirit is wounded, and he sees only the negative, the struggle ahead, and Ben's betrayal. Healing, both in body and mind, is a long arduous road.

It's up to Ben to convince Adam that there is still good in life and that he'll be there to help Adam every step of the way. If Adam will let him.

# http://www.harmonyinkpress.com

ROBBIE MICHAELS grew up in rural upstate New York, the same setting as the beginning of *The Most Popular Guy* books. It was not always easy growing up thinking he was the only gay person in the world. He felt like a stranger in a very strange land for most of those years, always having to act a part, play a role, until he later met other gay folks and found out that he was not alone. He was teased and bullied when others suspected that he might be gay. But he survived those days and found that life does get better, even though at the time it sure didn't seem possible. He wants first and foremost to tell others to hang on and to have hope for a better tomorrow. Life is a wonderful, marvelous thing to be embraced and celebrated. Don't ever give up. You are the only you there is. You are not alone. There are many, many, many others like you out there and some day you will meet them and together you will change the world in a wonderful, positive way. Please visit his website at http://www.robbiemichaels.com to learn more about his writing and to see his blog.

BOOK ONE:
THE MOST POPULAR GUY IN THE SCHOOL

The Most Popular Guy in the School

*Don't Judge a Book by its Cover*

ROBBIE MICHAELS

http://www.harmonyinkpress.com

BOOK TWO:
THE MOST POPULAR GUY IN THE SCHOOL

The Most Popular Guy in the School

Go West,
Young Man

ROBBIE MICHAELS

http://www.harmonyinkpress.com

BOOK THREE:
THE MOST POPULAR GUY IN THE SCHOOL

The Most Popular Guy in the School

*A Star is Born*

ROBBIE MICHAELS

http://www.harmonyinkpress.com

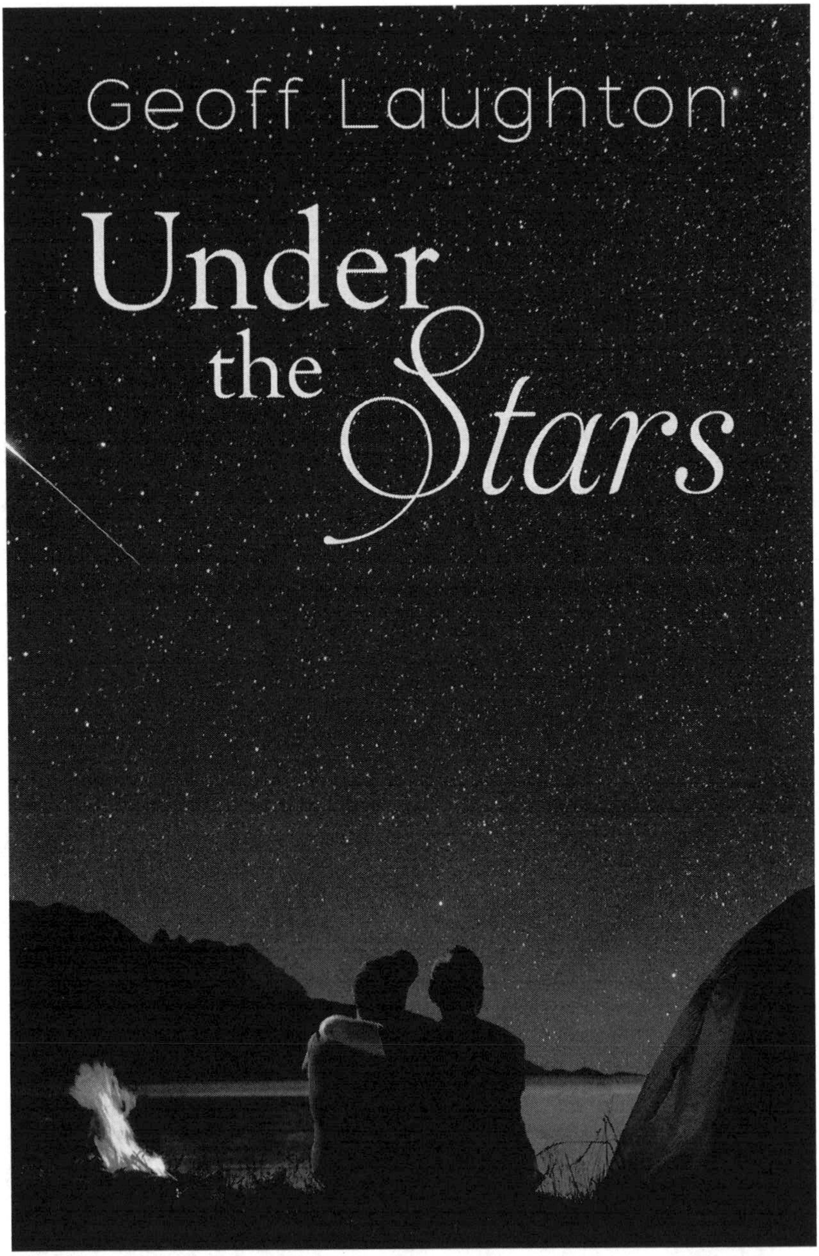


http://www.harmonyinkpress.com

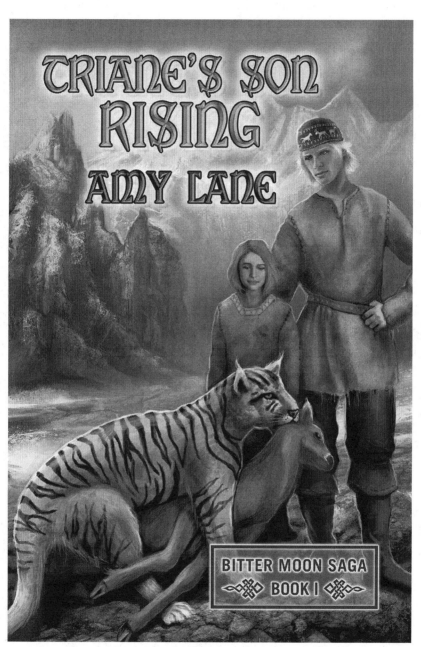

# TRIANE'S SON RISING
## AMY LANE

BITTER MOON SAGA
BOOK I

http://www.harmonyinkpress.com

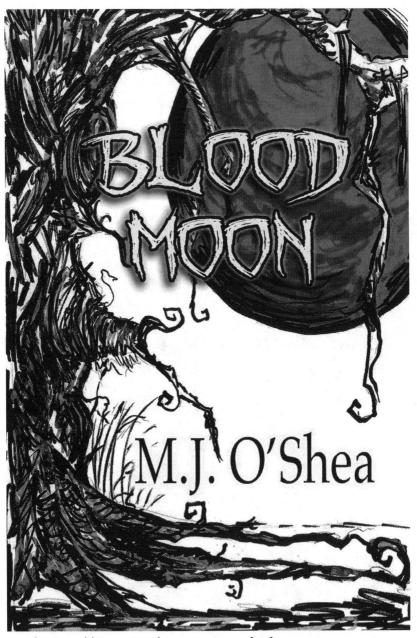

BLOOD
MOON

M.J. O'Shea

http://www.harmonyinkpress.com

JOHN GOODE

Straight    GAY    Straight    STRAIGHT

TALES FROM
FOSTER
HIGH

http://www.harmonyinkpress.com

*Nail Polish and Feathers*

Jo Ramsey

http://www.harmonyinkpress.com

BINARY BOY

RJ Astruc

http://www.harmonyinkpress.com

FOR MORE OF THE BEST LGBTQ+ YA FICTION

Harmony Ink

VISIT

HARMONYINKPRESS.COM